Scarred

BREAKING THE RULES SERIES
BOOK THREE

K. Webster

Dedication

To my mom who wasn't at all surprised when I became an author and said she always knew I'd do something really special. Thanks for never doubting my abilities.

Prologue

Olive

Two months earlier

"THAT'S A WRAP," James called out to me and the other two girls.

I was freaking out at the moment because Drake was glaring at me. Earlier, James had pulled my top down a little to "get the right shot." And even though it had been harmless, I could see that it was sending Drake over the edge. His eyes had grown stormy and furious.

His well-over-six-foot frame stood hulking off to the side staring menacingly at me. I cowered under his gaze and picked at my nail. *Tonight, I am going to pay for it.* A tear slipped out and I quickly wiped it away in an effort to not piss him off any further.

"Did you get some good shots?" James asked, walking over to Drake.

Drake dragged his gaze away from me down to his camera and started flipping through the photos to show James. They talked quietly and pointed out a few that they really liked. I felt sick to my stomach. Drake wouldn't let this go easily. He didn't like when men looked at me, but touching me was absolutely out of the question. A year of being together and I still didn't know how he would punish me this time.

When we first met, he'd been so dreamy. My extremely religious mother had disowned me when I'd expressed my wishes to model. After she warned me to never come back, I headed to New York to follow my dream. I was living in crummy conditions with a sketchy roommate, but it was something. It had hurt to leave my younger sister Opal, but I hoped that after some time had passed, my mother would allow me to see her again.

When Drake and I met at one of my first photo shoots, the air was charged with unique electricity. Immediately after the set, we ended up in the back of his car, where I painfully lost my virginity, but in that moment, it didn't matter. I'd fallen completely for the handsome devil. Our whirlwind romance began and I moved in with him right away.

At first, our relationship consisted of making love all hours of the day when we weren't working. It truly was perfect. But one day, something snapped in him. The sweet, romantic lover of mine turned into a monster. When he hit me for the first time, I was horrified and in shock. He apologized and begged for my forgiveness, but when it happened again a week later, I realized that was who he really was.

Drake became obsessed with controlling everything about me, down to what I ate and how much. He made my modeling schedule and decided which jobs I would take or not. When it came to sex, it was when he demanded it, wherever he demanded it. If I so much as fouled up a tiny bit, I would get punished.

He made sure to always hurt me where nobody would see the bruises since I was a model. When he kicked me, it was always on my back, my stomach, or my ribs. My breasts stayed bruised and sore.

I was dragged from my memories when I saw him stalking towards me. Instinctively, I wanted to flinch away from him but knew better. *God, tonight is going to be bad.*

"Let's get you home, Ollie," he growled, jerking my hand

roughly into his and hauling me out the door.

My heart started to race. Normally, he would wait until we got home to unleash his rage, but the fact that he could hardly keep it in check right now meant that it was going to be horrible when we got back to our apartment.

After we settled into his car, he started the engine but didn't move. Quick as lightning, he backhanded me across the face. I yelped in surprise and put my hand to my eye, which was stinging from the hit. *He never touches my face.* I couldn't even begin to fathom what he would do once we got home.

Will I even make it out alive this time?

As if sensing my fear, he pulled away and the door automatically locked.

The drive home was eerily quiet as I worried about what he would do. Once we arrived at the apartment, I considered bolting down the sidewalk, but he would only catch me and things would be even worse. Before I could act on my thoughts, his hand darted out and roughly gripped my bicep, hastily pulling me upstairs. My heart was pounding and I started to sob.

"Please, Drake. I'm so sorry. I had no idea he would touch me. It wasn't my fault," I explained as tears streamed shamelessly down my cheeks.

He unlocked the apartment door and shoved me inside. I stumbled forward but caught myself and spun around to face him. He had already locked the door behind him and was glaring at me as his chest heaved.

"Drake, if you love me, why do you hurt me?" I asked, stalling for time.

He laughed, one without humor, and it chilled my insides. "Ollie, I love you more than life. That's why I can't fucking stand to see anyone look at you, much less touch you. Your body belongs to me. You are my property. Why do you fucking flaunt yourself, practically begging for them to touch you?" he demanded angrily.

"Drake, please. I only love you. Can't you see that? Please don't hurt me. Come on, baby. Let's make love instead," I begged, trying to change his mind.

His expression softened, and I prayed he would back down. Hesitantly, I walked over to him and stood on my toes to kiss his lips. As if breaking from a trance, he met my kiss hungrily.

Grabbing my ass in both hands, he lifted me up to him. I wrapped my arms around his neck and my legs hooked his waist. He carried me into our bedroom and set me down on the bed. I quickly undressed for him while he pulled off his own clothes. After scooting farther up the bed, I lay back, waiting for his next move.

He never did mess around with foreplay anymore and immediately pounced on me. Lining himself up with my opening, he shoved himself in. I was completely dry, so I moaned out in pain but he thankfully thought it was in pleasure. Eventually, it didn't hurt anymore, and I rubbed his back, thinking that tomorrow I was going run away from him.

I could feel him about to come so I moaned louder beneath him. "I'm coming," I cried out, lying to him. His orgasm pumped into me and he collapsed on my chest.

Soon, I could hear him snoring. Tears silently fell down my face as I thanked God for the bullet I had just dodged.

I awoke to my arm being pulled roughly. Alarmed, I looked over to see Drake tying my arm to the bedpost. My other arm and legs had already been secured. After he finished, he looked at me hatefully. *Crap.* He swayed a little, which meant he had been drinking. *Crap, crap, crap!* He forced a rolled-up sock into my mouth and I tried not to gag. My eyes pled with him.

"I'm tired of them looking at you. You're my property, Ollie. Can't you see that? It's time for there to never be a question ever again," he spat cryptically.

Tears were a steady stream now as I wriggled to no avail. When he pulled a knife from the bedside table, I started shuddering as sobs racked my body.

Straddling my naked body, he slowly dragged the knife across my belly, tickling the flesh. Goose bumps spread over my skin. My chest was heaving wildly as I feared what he was about to do.

Without any warning, he dug the knife into the flesh of my belly underneath my breasts. I screamed into the sock in agony as he carved my skin. He was quiet and determined, immune to my muffled wailing. It felt like he was slicing a word across my stomach. My vision was blurry as the pain threatened to make me pass out. I worried that, if I did, he would finish the job and kill me.

He stopped for a moment and I cried out, relieved for a reprieve from the pain. Then just below, he began carving again, but this time a shorter word. My body was drenched in sweat but a shiver kept running over me.

When he started again, the knife dug into the flesh below my belly button and I screamed through the shock. It hurt worse in that supersensitive area and I actually blacked out momentarily. When I came back to, he was standing beside me, checking out his handiwork. He pulled the sock from my mouth and I immediately felt bile rising in my throat.

"Drake, I am about to be sick," I choked out right before I start gagging.

He quickly untied me and carried me to the bathroom. I barely made it to the toilet before I start vomiting. This went on until I was dry heaving stomach acid. I heard him exit the bathroom.

I was afraid to inspect the damage across my torso. It hurt so much, but all I could think about was how I was going to escape from here alive. My body collapsed to the floor and I shivered again uncontrollably. His feet appeared in my line of vision and I flinched.

A sudden kick to my stomach had me howling in pain. *I can't take any more of this from him!* Thankfully, the kick was the only one he delivered and he stumbled back to the bedroom. I tried to sit up, but a sharp pain ripped through my lower belly. When I looked down, I noticed that I was bleeding everywhere from the cuts. I needed to get to a hospital soon.

Summoning some strength, I crawled towards the bathroom door and peeked my head out. He was sprawled out face-first on the bed, snoring. I shakily pulled myself to my feet but doubled over from the pain, grabbing the doorframe to keep from falling. I shuffled over to my clothes and put them on as fast as I could, pausing every few seconds to breathe deeply through the agonizing burn both outside and in my belly.

When he groaned, I almost yelped in fear but continued my task by finally slipping on my shoes. I hobbled into the living room, pulling my coat on and grabbing my purse. The door closed behind me, and I half-ran, half-stumbled in the direction of the hospital.

"Miss Redding?" a gentle voice asked, pulling me from a deep sleep.

I blinked my eyes open to see an older woman with kind eyes staring over me.

Where am I?

"Sweetie, I'm Dr. Winston. Can you tell me what happened to you?" she asked softly.

My eyes darted around the room and I sighed in relief when

I noticed that he wasn't there. I must have made it to the hospital somehow.

"Um, my boyfriend hurt me," I choked out, tears forming in my eyes.

"Yes, young lady. He certainly did. Is there someone we can call?" she asked.

I shook my head sadly, which caused her to frown. She pulled my hand into her own and looked at me with such compassion. My heart nearly broke in half.

"Miss Redding, we cleaned the lacerations and stitched up the deep ones but I'm afraid you'll have some scarring," she sighed.

I didn't care at this point because I was free from him.

She bit her lip as she contemplated her next words. Her hand quickly squeezed mine. "And I'm afraid you lost the baby," she told me.

Baby? What baby? "I'm sorry but I wasn't pregnant," I informed her. Her frown told me I was wrong.

"Honey, you were just two months along, but trauma to your abdomen, most likely from a kick, caused you to miscarry. I'm so sorry," she whispered, squeezing my hand again.

Tears slipped out as I mourned the loss of an innocent being. *A being I couldn't protect.* My sobs took over and Dr. Winston enveloped me in a motherly hug, making me mourn the loss of my own mom as well.

The hospital released me the very next day, and I limped along, wondering where I would go. Feeling very winded, I slipped into a café and sat down at the first table. Tears start falling down my face and I tried viciously to stop them to no avail. When a blond-haired beauty took the seat in front of me, I couldn't help but look at her.

"Babe, you look like shit. Are you okay?" she asked gently. When I shook my head, she scooted her chair beside me and pulled me in for a hug.

Who is this sweet stranger?

"I'm going to make you my special coffee and get you some soup. You stay right here," she instructed and bounced off, going behind the counter. Moments later, she brought me what she promised. "Now spill, sweetie," she gently instructed me.

I took a few bites of my soup. "Well, my boyfriend hurt me. Really, really hurt me. I've managed to escape from him. Now I'm trying to figure out my next move," I explained sadly.

Decision crossed her features as she prepared herself for her next words. "You're coming home with me. My roommate and I have an extra room. You don't have to pay us anything. Honey, we're going to take care of you," she assured me matter-of-factly.

Tears formed again and I nodded. I wanted nothing more than for this sweet, angelic girl to take care of me.

"I'm Andi," my heroine said, finally introducing herself.

"Olive," I greeted back, smiling a genuine smile for the first time in quite some time.

She grabbed my hand and our friendship began.

Chapter ONE

Bray

"**I WANT YOU** to come to my party tomorrow night," Andi declared genuinely from the chair on the other side of my desk.

I took a moment to admire her beauty. Her long blond hair was ironed perfectly straight today and had an ethereal glow to it. I'd forever punish myself for that one stupid fuck-up last spring.

"Ugh, I don't know. Your boyfriend hates me," I reminded her, crossing my arms as I leaned back in my chair.

She frowned and her bottom lip stuck out a little. "Please, Bray. Dr. Sweeney thinks it would be best if you and I could learn to be friends. Friends go to each other's birthday parties. He also said Jackson especially needed to make an effort with you."

Today she was wearing a button-up blouse with the first two undone, allowing her cleavage to peek out. *I made her this way.* My weak moment with that bimbo Steph from college had turned Andi into this woman I hardly knew. It almost seemed like punishment to have to work with her every day while she was scantily dressed, fucking the guy in the office next door. *But I deserve it.*

Sighing, I finally smiled at her and she squealed in excitement. The way her face lit up reminded me of a time when we were once together, making my heart physically hurt from the memory.

"Yeah, Andi. I'll be there. I know I'm looking forward to hanging out with my buddies Pepper and Jackson," I teased.

Sticking her tongue at me, she tossed a folder at me and papers spilled out over my lap. "Ha! That's what you get for being a dick. Just come on over after work. Do you remember how to get there?" she questioned and her cheeks immediately reddened.

It wasn't long ago that I'd falsely hoped we would get back together. We'd both been hot and heavy for each other until she called me Jackson. *Kind of killed the mood.* But for as much as I was wounded, I really only wanted her to be happy. Even if that meant she was with another man.

"Yeah, I'll be there," I promised and she bounced out of my office. Shaking my head, I dove back into my work.

The newest design I was working on was a tricky one. A developer wanted to tear down an existing building and erect a state-of-the-art apartment complex complete with a parking garage. The problem was space. The area I had to work with was long and unusually narrow. I had almost figured out how it could work and still be badass like my client had requested.

When my cell rang, I cringed when I saw it was my mother. If I ignored it, she would just keep calling until I answered. And if I answered, I would be stuck on the phone for quite a while with her. Either way, it was always a pain when she called me during my workday. Deciding to just get it over with, I swiped it to accept the call.

"Hey, Mom," I answered as I continued to work on my computer, tweaking my design.

"Bray, how are you doing today?" she asked happily into the phone. Her tone was a little too chipper, and I braced myself for what was coming.

"I'm doing fine, Mother. Work has been super busy and I'm trying to finish up a project for one of my clients. Did you need something?"

"How's Andi doing?" she asked, cutting to the chase. This was where the conversation went almost every single time we talked.

"Andi is fine. She just invited me to her party tomorrow," I told her, hoping she would move on to other topics. I rolled my eyes when she squawked on the other line.

"Oh, Bray! I knew you two would work it out. Tell her I love and miss her."

"Mom, I'm going as a friend. She has a new boyfriend now, remember? They love each other."

"Oh crumbs! I was afraid of that. That's why I went ahead and set up a dinner tonight for you to meet my bridge club friend's daughter Kacey."

"I wish you would stop trying to do stuff like that. You know I hate going on these blind dates," I grumbled to her. When she started sniffling on the other line, I instantly felt guilty for having been harsh with her. I was such a damn Momma's boy.

"Son, I just want you to be happy. If it isn't going to be with Andi, I think you should move on and start dating again. You haven't dated anyone since she broke up with you. I still don't understand how, after four years of being together, she could dump her fiancé so suddenly," she complained.

The guilt washed over me like it did every time we had this conversation. I'd never told my mom about the chick I'd fucked in a moment of stupidity. She still thought I was her perfect son who was dumped by his would-be wife.

"I know, Mom. That sounds good. Where do I need to meet this Kacey?" I asked. There was no point in avoiding the inevitable now. Might as well try it out and see. Eventually, I would get over Andi, even though it was really fucking hard when she bounded into my office all day every day.

"Thank you, honey. I'll text you her number so you can set

something up with her. Good luck, and let me know how it goes."

"Love you, Mom."

"So what do you do for a living?" I asked Kacey after the server had left to put in our order. She was really pretty, but there hadn't been an instant connection. I felt myself counting down the minutes until it was over, but unfortunately, our date had only just begun. Sometimes I could be such a dick.

"I'm an esthetician. There's a pretty swanky spa near here that caters to a ritzy crowd. You have to put up with some snobs, but the tips are great," she revealed, smiling brightly at me. My eyes flitted down to her breasts, which were practically spilling out of her top, before they made their way back to her face again.

"Sounds cool. So, uh, do you have any siblings?" I questioned in an attempt to keep the conversation going. So far, she would answer my question and then smile at me as if waiting for another one. You'd think she was a contestant at the Miss America pageant.

"Nope, just me." And there it was again—the expectant look and pearly white smile.

I refrained from rolling my eyes. Instead, my eyes dropped back down to her chest. There hadn't been anyone since that slut from six months ago and, before that, Andi. My dick was starting to feel neglected. Surely I could just allow myself a pity fuck.

"Let's see… Tell me what you like to do," I solicited, hoping for more information this time. While she talked about yoga, I looked at her breasts again. They slightly bounced as she animatedly spoke about crouching dragon poses or some shit. Her tits were perky, and she was definitely flaunting them for me. I could totally fuck her. The problem would be getting rid of her afterwards. It would definitely only be a one-time thing.

After what seemed like a really long dinner, I wondered if I could casually have sex with this girl. Casual sex wasn't normally my thing, but I was starting to think I could learn.

Kacey definitely wanted me based on the way she batted her eyelashes and giggled every few minutes. On the way back to drop her off, I continued to try to converse with her to no avail. She happily answered any questions I threw at her but didn't ask one single question of me. I was used to Andi. The thought of her made my heart clench painfully.

What the hell am I doing?

In the end, I decided against my dick's wishes. There was no way I'd ever be into a girl like Kacey, so there wasn't any point in leading her on. When I pulled up in front of her building but made no attempt to turn off the car or get out, she looked over and frowned.

"I had a nice night," I lied.

Her eyes lit up and she smiled broadly. Leaning over, she pecked me on the cheek, but I didn't turn to meet her kiss. I could sense the rejection she felt, which in turn made me feel like an ass.

I thought she would pull away and leave, but instead, her hand cupped my cock through my jeans, which made me jump in surprise.

"Kacey, what are you doing?" I inquired, my dick growing hard underneath her hand.

Instead of answering me, she undid the top button of my jeans and slid down the zipper. My cock betrayed me as it fought wildly to escape my boxer briefs. They must have been on the same team because she freed it, taking it into her mouth. I groaned as my hands went automatically to her hair.

Kacey wasn't good at small talk but the girl could suck dick. I clutched her hair as she bobbed wildly up and down. When she took it deep in her throat, I came unexpectedly and she choked a little before swallowing it down. Pulling away, she pecked me again on my cheek and hopped out of the car.

That was the last time I ever saw Kacey.

Chapter TWO

Olive

THE CAKE WAS chocolate—Andi's favorite. That girl had a passion for food and was surprisingly rail-thin. I put the cake, still in the box, in the middle of the table and went back over to check the mail. There was a check from my last modeling job. Every check that came through, I tried to send most of it to Momma. She might not have wanted to talk to me anymore, but I knew how poor she was, and every little bit would help her.

Pepper would be back at any time, so I figured I better get ready for the party. I dug around my closet until I found a dressy pair of grey shorts and a black dolman top. When I pulled off my t-shirt, I stepped in front of the mirror to look at my scars. They were a daily reminder that I had survived a horrific situation that had taken the life of my baby and nearly my own. Tears filled my eyes and I quickly batted them away.

"Olive? Are you here?" Pepper shouted from the entryway.

I tore my eyes away from the horrible scarring on my abdomen, tossed my shirt on, and slipped on my flats. "I'm in here babe," I called to her, stepping out of my bedroom.

She met me there and gave me a huge hug. Ever since Pepper had met Jordan, she'd been a new woman. I'd never seen her so carefree and happy before. Those two were a perfect match. Between Andi and Pepper both finding love, I couldn't help but feel a pang of jealousy.

Walking back into the kitchen, she was all business.

"Did you get the cake?" she asked.

I smiled at her and pointed at the table. "I got her favorite—chocolate. When will everyone get here?" I inquired. Being a homebody meant that I thrived on hanging out with my girlfriends. And as nervous as I was for the guys to be there, it was also sort of exciting. I still felt bad that Andi had decided to have her party at home rather than at a bar or someplace. She always considered my needs unselfishly.

"Everyone will be here after work. They should be showing up anytime. Lucky for you, tonight you get to meet Andi's ex-dickhead. I hate that her stupid shrink is encouraging this friendship. Dr. Sweeney wasn't fucking there when she almost died because of Bray's ass," she spat angrily.

Pepper hated Bray and so did I. We'd never met before, but she'd told me countless stories of their awful breakup and his infidelity. He was lucky he would even get to step foot in our apartment. Pepper really loved Andi to honor her wishes because I knew she absolutely hated Bray.

Someone knocked on the door and Pepper went over to answer it. "Fucking Bray," she muttered only loud enough for me to hear. I was strangely eager to see this notorious guy who'd hurt my best friend so badly.

Bray stepped into the apartment and my belly flopped. I cursed myself but couldn't help but stare. He was absolutely gorgeous. The man was tall and muscular, and he had dark-blond hair that was styled to look messy.

"Just put it over here," she ordered, glaring at him.

He frowned as he passed her. His eyes lifted to meet mine, and my stomach felt jittery when he smiled the most breathtaking smile at me.

My knees felt shaky underneath me as his eyes blatantly skirted up my body. I felt naked under his gaze and fought back a shiver. No matter how hot he was or how badly I wanted to stare at him all day, it couldn't happen. Andi was my best friend, and this could in no way ever evolve into anything.

Pepper said something snide to him and I brought myself out of the spell my mind had gone under.

"Nice to meet you. I'm Bray," he greeted me, still grinning. He held out his hand for me to shake.

Afraid I wouldn't let go, I kept my hands clasped together in front of me and smiled tightly at him. His smile fell and I immediately felt my heart drop. There was something magnetic about him, and I felt sick to my stomach for allowing myself to be drawn to it.

"You too," I clipped out and bolted into the kitchen away from his dangerously gorgeous face. I tried to busy myself with pulling the cake out of the box and putting it on the table. If Bray was going to be hanging around us more often, I was going to have to get my hormones in check. Andi would be devastated if she saw the way I'd been drooling over him. *This is so bad.*

"Olive, contrary to what Andi and Pepper may have told you, I'm not a bad guy," he murmured from behind me.

My body betrayed me as tingles tore across my skin just from the sound of his voice. Whirling around, I nearly gasped when I saw his beautiful form leaning against the counter. His tight Henley shirt stretched across every curve of every muscle. Peeling my eyes away from his chiseled body, I brought my gaze to his. He was smiling warmly at me.

I had spent the last few months avoiding people, especially men, because of the horrors Drake had caused me. Every man that looked at me made me feel like prey. But Bray? He just made me feel like I was on the menu—but in a good way—and I was conflicted by those feelings since he was clearly Andi's horrible ex-fiancé.

"Bray, all I've heard are bad things. How can you come in here and act like you didn't nearly ruin Andi's life?" I questioned in nearly a whisper, not trusting my voice to go any louder for fear of it shaking.

His bright grin fell and he rubbed his palms across his stubbly cheeks in frustration. "What I did with Andi was wrong and I'll always carry that with me, but I am not a bad guy. I made a mistake. One mistake."

Dragging my eyes from his, I turned back to the cake. He was completely beautiful, but I had standards. Crushing over my best friend's ex was not something I could do. *Ever.*

"Fine, Bray. Let's try to be friends since Andi clearly wants us to be," I sighed as I turned to look at him again. The way he stared at me, with such unmasked desire, made my stomach flip once again.

"What if I want to be more than just friends?" he asked, one eyebrow cocking up. My face burned with embarrassment at his blatant insinuation.

"Make yourself useful and help me put out all of the food," Pepper barked at him when she walked into the kitchen.

I was saved from his blazing stare and grabbed the bags from her. Bray came over and started opening boxes with me.

"Jordan! Cut it out!" Pepper screamed at Jordan, who'd just come in and hauled her out of the room.

Once again, I was left alone with Bray. Well, so much for that.

"Those shorts are nice on you, but I need to ask. Why in the world are you wearing shorts in November?" he chuckled. His voice was smooth, and it melted my insides. I hoped my reaction to him wasn't as noticeable as it felt. If so, I would be in trouble with both Andi and Pepper.

"I like shorts and I'm inside. What does it matter?" I retorted. He smiled that panty-dropping grin of his and lazily dragged his gaze down my legs again. My heart fluttered as I watched him.

"I like shorts too," he agreed as his eyes met mine. The humor was gone and his gaze was full of heat, probably matching my own.

Jordan walked back into the kitchen looking much like the cat that ate the canary. Bray looked at him quizzically. Moments later, Pepper followed him into the room, her skin flushed. Those two had obviously just gotten freaky. Bray grinned at me as if noticing as well, and I couldn't help but return his smile. That smile of his was going to get me in a lot of trouble.

Chapter THREE

Bray

OLIVE WAS A LONG-LEGGED beauty, and I wanted her the instant I saw her. Her face was incredibly expressive, and I could see that she was attracted to me but fought it wildly because I was Andi's notorious ex-fiancé.

Andi and Jackson came through the front door, causing both Pepper and Olive to squeal as they ran over to wish her a happy birthday. Jackson moved past them to join Jordan and me in the kitchen.

"You guys need a drink?" he asked, rolling his eyes at the girls' noisy chatter. We both nodded and he made his way over to the bottle of Jack Daniel's on the counter.

"How come you guys never told me Andi and Pepper's room-mate Olive was a freaking goddess?" I asked Jackson and Jordan. My question immediately earned me a glare from Jackson, who'd spun around from his task, nearly knocking over the bottle in the process.

"Bray, leave her the fuck alone. She's a fragile girl, and you tend to leave a path of destruction wherever you go," he spat at me.

"What the fuck is everyone's problem? Did you and Pepper

place bets on who could be the biggest ass to me?" I asked him angrily.

He visibly tensed, and I wondered if I would get a chance to punch him in his jaw tonight. The guy rubbed every nerve I had the wrong way. Clearly I had the same effect on him.

"You two need to chill out before Andi gets pissed. Let's eat," Jordan said quickly in an effort to keep things from escalating. Jackson was lucky his brother was a good guy. Because of my respect for Jordan, I refrained from going off on Jackson like I really wanted to.

Everyone grabbed seats around the table. Olive reluctantly sat down in the empty chair beside me. When her knee accidentally bumped against mine under the table, she jerked it away and looked over at me. I just grinned at her and threw her a wink. Her cheeks reddened and she quickly looked away. It amazed me that someone with mocha-colored skin could blush so noticeably.

Dinner went great and everyone conversed easily. While everyone was having cake and teasing Andi over her love for food, I took the moment to look over at Olive again. She smiled happily at Andi. Olive was so damn attractive. Her brown skin was absolutely flawless, the perfect shade of milk chocolate, and damn if I didn't want to taste it. As if on cue, she peeked over at me again. I could tell she couldn't keep her eyes off me any more easily than I could from her.

"What?" she mouthed to me as to not bring attention to our exchange.

I studied her pouty lips a moment before answering. "Do you really want to know?" I teased. Her impossibly light brown eyes narrowed as she tried to determine if she really wanted to know or not. Finally, she gave in to her curiosity and nodded.

Leaning over close to her, I pulled the hair away from her ear, dragging my fingers across her neck in the process. She shivered but didn't move away. Her lips parted as she waited for my answer.

"I was just thinking I wanted to have a little nibble of you to see if you really do taste like chocolate," I answered, my hot breath in her ear.

"Are you guys ready for presents?" she asked suddenly, jumping up from her seat. Her cheeks were flushed and she avoided eye contact with me. I was confident she wouldn't be immune to my charms for much longer.

After Andi announced that we should all get drunk once she'd opened her presents, we all did just that. Olive was stuck between the arm of the sofa and me. She wasn't making any moves to pull away, which I took to be a good sign. Everyone was feeling the effects of the alcohol and were pretty much sticking to each other. Since Olive and I were the only single ones, it was only natural for us to hang out together.

"How tall are you?" I asked her, not taking my eyes from her sweet lips. She smiled, showing her perfect white teeth, and I suddenly felt the need to kiss her but refrained.

"I'm five foot eleven. They seem to like my height at the agency," she confirmed.

I nodded, and my eyes swept over her bare legs again for the hundredth time of the night. Her thin, long legs were divine, and I couldn't seem to get enough of them. As the alcohol warmed us both, she didn't seem to be holding herself back as much or embarrassed by my overt ogling. In fact, she seemed to enjoy it.

"Olive, you're so beautiful. Why are you trying so hard to resist me?" I questioned as I stroked my pinky along the outside of her thigh. Andi and Jackson had already moved on to her room, and from the corner of my eye, I'd seen Jordan scoop up Pepper and take her to her room. Finally, I had Olive alone.

"Because, Bray, it's wrong for me to like you. You are my best friend's ex. And in case you've forgotten, she almost lost her life because of the depression she endured from your infidelity. The list of reasons to hate you is a mile high," she informed me. Even though her words said one thing, her body told me another as it shivered at my touch.

"It may be wrong, but you still want me. I will forever be pissed at myself for that moment of stupidity and the horror I caused Andi, but I have to go on and live my life at some point. She's happy now. Why can't I be?" I asked, genuinely wanting to know the answer.

Olive frowned, which made her bottom lip poke out. I really wanted to suck that lip into my mouth. She turned to look at me and I had a hard time not doing just that.

"You can be happy, Bray. Just not with me. What would it do to Andi if she knew I was completely hot for her ex-fiancé?" she asked sadly. I grinned at her, which ultimately caused the corners of her lips to tilt up in a smile.

"You're hot for me?" I teased. Her cheeks turned red and the lip poked out again.

"Yes, I am, and it totally sucks because it can't happen, Bray," she told me firmly.

It was my turn to frown. "What can't happen, Olive? Sex? I just want to kiss you. Don't you want to kiss me? That's all we'll do," I promised. When she didn't respond, I leaned forward until my lips were almost touching hers. Her eyes fluttered closed, giving me the permission I needed. I pressed my lips to hers and she melted to me.

Our kiss started out sweet, lips only. I was finally able to suck that plump lip into my mouth, and it tasted better than I'd imagined. When she moaned and parted her mouth, I slipped my tongue into her mouth where her own met mine. The innocent kiss turned into a needy, hungry one.

I brought a hand to her face and gently stroked her cheek. Her tiny hands slid up to my shoulders, tentatively touching me. Needing her closer to me, I dragged her over into my lap. She yelped in surprise but quickly made herself comfortable as she straddled my lap.

We continued to kiss deeply. Neither one of us made any moves to progress any further than what we were doing even though we both clearly wanted more. The way she was grinding herself into my hard cock, which was pressed against my jeans, was a distinct indication of just how much she wanted me.

My hands slithered up and down her back. I wanted so badly to rip her clothes off and fuck her right then. As if realizing I wanted to push things further, she pulled away, breathing heavily.

"Bray, we should stop," she panted unconvincingly.

"Do you want to stop, Olive?" I asked, thrusting my hips upwards.

Her eyes closed again as she allowed me to press myself into her.

"Olive, I want to taste you—everywhere," I practically begged as she rode me through my clothes, meeting me thrust for thrust. I cupped her small breasts through her top and she moaned again. Slipping a hand down, I thumbed her clit through her shorts and she melted to me.

"Yes, Bray, yes," she pleaded as her breathing intensified.

Not waiting her to change her mind, I stood up with her and her legs wrapped around my hips as she held on. I sort of half-stumbled towards the only open bedroom door and she giggled. If we felt bad about this later, we could blame it on being drunk.

"Leave the lights off," she commanded once we stepped into her room.

Obeying her, I shut and locked the door behind us and set her down. She grabbed my hand and led me blindly to her bed. I felt her hands reach for the bottom of my shirt and pull it over my head. Two tiny hands slid over my chest, feeling each groove between my muscles. They finally made their way down and unfastened my jeans. I helped her slide them down and groaned when both of her hands gripped my cock.

"You're so big," she praised, stroking it.

Needing to touch her, I grabbed her head and pulled her to me for another deep kiss. I kicked off my jeans the rest of the way along with my shoes. Reaching behind her, I cupped her small, round ass.

"I need to be inside you. Now," I growled and yanked off her shirt. She yelped in surprise but didn't push me away.

One quick unhook of her bra and her perky tits were free. I leaned down, sucking one into my mouth, and she purred like a fucking kitten. My hands found the top of her shorts and got them off of her in record speed. The tiny shred of material that were her panties disappeared an instant later.

I slid a hand down and cupped her sex. She was smoothly shaven down there, and I nearly came from the idea of it.

"I want to see you," I mumbled as I began stroking her between her folds. She moaned but made no moves to turn on a lamp.

"No, please," she answered nervously.

Something about the tone of her voice made me drop the subject. I quickened the pace of my finger and she was soon shuddering around me as an orgasm coursed through her.

Chapter FOUR

Olive

ALL SANITY WENT out the window once Bray and I had crossed the line by kissing. Now I was about to have sex with the man who'd nearly ruined my best friend and I didn't care in that heated moment. It made me a total bitch, but all I could think about was him. He enchanted me with his voice, his body, his taste, *his scent*. How in the world could he break through and make me feel desired and safe? Feeling safe was definitely a new feeling for me.

"Bray, I want you so bad," I whispered against his lips.

His strong arms lifted me up and my legs wrapped instinctively around him. I felt him guide his cock to my entrance, and once the tip was in the right place, I pushed myself down onto it. We both gasped at the sensation. He was huge but I was wet and easily slid over him.

Once settled, with his massive arms he bounced me up and down his length. Both of his large hands gripped my ass as he guided me at a pace we both enjoyed. My arms were locked around his neck, holding on for dear life.

When he stumbled again, causing me to giggle loudly, I realized we were pretty drunk, and having sex this way was probably dangerous.

"Put me on the bed," I purred, pulling his lip into my mouth. He complied, and we soon picked up our pace once again.

Drake had given me a few orgasms in our time together but never once while he was inside me. My heart pounded as I realized I was about to have another one with Bray. Electric tingles slid down my body right to my core. The shudders that suddenly convulsed through my body were violent and exquisite all the same.

"Bray," I moaned as a tear slipped out of my eye. Moments later, I felt him spill his own orgasm into me. He collapsed on me, breathing heavily. I threaded my fingers through his hair and scratched his scalp.

"Mmmm," he groaned appreciatively. Wanting to keep him happy, I continued until his soft snores eventually lulled me to sleep as well.

It was still dark when I awoke to kisses on my neck. Bray was growing hard within me, and when he realized I was awake, he started slowly sliding in and out.

"You feel so good, Olive," he murmured into my neck. I could feel another orgasm creeping up, and I sighed happily.

"So do you, Bray. Go faster," I urged. He picked up the pace and we both came together moments later.

Rolling us over to where I was on top, he gently stroked my back. I curled up to his hard chest and enjoyed the sweet closeness that was something Drake and I had never shared. We once again fell asleep in each other's arms.

The morning light shone through the window waking me up. My head throbbed violently as I tried to recall the events from last night. A groan from beside me made me swivel my head towards the sound. The beautiful naked form that was Bray lay sprawled out beside me, a big muscular arm tossed across my scarred belly. Something about the sight of his arm stretched over the nasty engraving jerked me from my stupor. *Crap!*

What in the hell have we done? This was Andi's ex for crying out loud. *What kind of bitch am I?* I slipped out from underneath him and ran to the bathroom in my room, yanking my robe over me. Stalking back into the room, I shook his massive body.

"Bray, get up!" I hissed, not wanting to wake anyone else in the apartment.

He groaned and patted the bed beside him. "Olive, come back to bed and cuddle with me," he grunted, his voice thick with sleep.

"Get up. Seriously, like now. If Andi finds out about this, she'll hate me. Now get up, please," I begged, tears forming in my eyes. He must have heard the desperation in my voice because he turned over to look at me, his eyes red and squinting.

"Fuck," he mumbled, realization kicking in. I hurried to the other side of the bed and picked up his clothes, tossing them at him.

"Hurry," I pleaded. This time, the tears won over.

He quickly put his clothes on and came over to where I was standing. "Olive, when can I see you again?" he asked, wiping a tear from my cheek.

I shook my head and took a step back, needing to avoid his close proximity. "Bray, never. We can't do this again, ever. Please don't make this any harder than it needs to be. We were drunk and stupid."

He frowned at my words and gently wiped another tear away.

"We'll talk to her. Andi is reasonable and happy with Jackson now. She'll understand. She will want you to be happy," he reasoned with me.

"No, I won't do that to her. Now get out," I ordered, anger lacing my voice.

28

"Olive—" he began, but I interrupted him by pushing him away from me.

"Get. Out," I hissed, pointing at the door. I was being a complete bitch, but I couldn't risk Andi or Pepper seeing him in my room.

Shaking his head, he slipped on his shoes and stalked out of the bedroom. Moments later, I heard the front door slam shut. Sinking to my bed, I cried my eyes out for the rest of the afternoon because of my betrayal to my best friend.

Chapter FIVE

Bray

LAST NIGHT WITH Olive had been amazing. The fact that she wanted to end it before it had even begun because of what Andi and Pepper might think pissed me off. For Olive to ignore the chemistry we had… I was left dumbfounded.

I spent the entire day at work trying to figure out how to convince her to give us a shot. At one point, I almost blurted it out to Andi. I was almost sure she would be okay with it. But the fact that Olive was worried about her reaction made me refrain from dropping that bomb on her without Olive's permission.

Several times I looked at my phone but realized I couldn't call or text her since we hadn't traded numbers. Finally, I decided I would take a chance and swing by the apartment later. Andi was talking about going to dinner later with Jackson and his mom. Jordan and Pepper had the gala. I hoped I could catch her by herself so we could talk.

After a busy day at work, I picked up some Chinese takeout on the way to her place. When she answered the door, her face was one of shock and pleasant surprise. The latter of which she quickly masked away.

"Can we talk?" I asked her, holding up the takeout. She eyed it suspiciously but finally, reluctantly, nodded.

I followed her in and couldn't take my eyes from her ass in the cotton shorts that barely covered it. Her long brown legs stretched out underneath them all the way to her bare feet. She turned to face me once we made it into the kitchen. The tight white tank top revealed that she wasn't wearing a bra, and I felt myself growing hard at the sight.

"What is there to talk about?" she asked nervously as she crossed her arms over her chest ending my peep show.

Dragging my eyes back to her face, I frowned. "Olive, I want to see you again. We have undeniable chemistry. Let's see where it takes us. I haven't felt this pull to someone since…" I stupidly trailed off.

She looked down, and that damn pouty lip jutted out. "Since Andi," she finished for me. "Bray, she's my best friend. I can't do this. We had a one-night stand. End of story." Her chin quivered slightly, and I suddenly felt like an asshole.

"I'm sorry, Olive. I don't want to hurt Andi either. Believe it or not, I care about her. But I also can't deny what we had last night," I proclaimed. Her eyes flicked up to mine, and they held uncertainty in them this time. Taking advantage of her indecision, I walked up to her, leaving only a couple of inches between us. Her breathing became heavy at our closeness.

Leaning forward, I captured her mouth with mine, and she dissolved into my embrace. Her arms snaked around my neck as I kissed her deeply, pushing her back against the counter. Lifting her onto the counter, I quickly unfastened my slacks, letting them drop to the floor. Her eyes dropped to my cock, which was begging to be let free from my boxers, and she bit her bottom lip. I pulled it out and stroked it once before reaching over and sliding her shorts to the side, giving me a prime view of her smooth pussy. Dipping my head, I licked her between the folds and she nearly bucked herself off the counter.

"You like that?" I asked her, looking up from under my lashes at her. She nodded vigorously.

Her eyes were closed, her head tilted back. When I licked her again, her mouth parted and she whimpered. I tongued her again, finding just the spot that made her jump, this time paying special attention to it. After only a short while of sucking and tasting it, she came wildly, moaning my name.

Not wasting any time, I squatted and reached into the pocket of my pants, located a condom, and quickly put it on. Her legs were still quivering from her orgasm. Pulling her to the edge of the counter, I once again pulled her shorts to the side and slammed into her.

"Oh God, Bray!" she shouted as I began pounding into her. Her fingers found my hair and pulled a little roughly. When I started to pull her tank top off, she nearly jumped off the counter from trying to stop me. She was self-conscious about something. It couldn't be her weight—she was perfectly thin. I settled for nibbling her nipple through the thin material of her tank.

When I felt her already tight pussy clenching around my cock with her orgasm, I lost control and came immediately. After a few seconds, I pulled away from her.

"Tell me that wasn't amazing," I teased, causing her to grin back at me.

"It was okay," she joked and looked at her fingernail, feigning boredom.

Laughing at her, I tickled her ribs, making her squeal.

"Cut it out, Bray!" she shrieked.

Grabbing hold of her hands, I helped her off the counter. I dropped the condom into the trashcan and pulled my pants back up. While she ran off to the bathroom to clean up, I washed my hands and made my way over to the bag of food.

"You hungry?" I asked once she returned, and I opened the boxes and set them on the counter.

She nodded and pulled some plates from the cabinet. After we sat down to eat, she spoke again.

"Bray? How will this work? I can't tell her," she uttered sadly as she ate.

"Why don't we try? I think you're worrying more about it than she will," I answered honestly. I saw the way Andi and Jackson were. Our relationship was most definitely a thing of the past.

"No. I can't tell her. Bray, I am a horrible friend," she said tearfully.

I reached over and took hold of her hand. "Olive, we won't tell her until you're ready. If you want to hide it from her, fine. I don't feel comfortable sneaking around, but I'll take what I can get at this point," I agreed. She smiled at me, and it was one of relief.

"Thanks. I promise, I'll tell her when the time is right."

I had a feeling that not telling Andi from the beginning might end up backfiring on us.

Chapter SIX

Olive

HE'D COME BACK. I was a terrible person for what we were doing, but I didn't want to stop. Bray made me feel things I'd never felt with Drake before. All of my insecurities and fears seemed to vanish when I was around him—well, almost all of them. Because of this, I selfishly wanted him even though I knew it would hurt Andi. There had to be away to have Bray without hurting her. In the meantime, I would hide our relationship from both her and Pepper. Where Andi would be upset, Pepper would be pissed. Pissed Pepper was a scary thought.

"Olive, I want to take you out. Do you want to go get drinks or something?" he asked after we tossed or leftovers into the trash. I frowned because, even though we were drawn together almost by an invisible magnetic field, we didn't know the first thing about one another. He had no idea about my social anxiety, fearing that I'd run into Drake publically.

"Um, Bray, let's take things slow. Maybe another day. I want to hang out here tonight while we have the place to ourselves," I told him, trying to avoid the subject.

He studied me for a moment before nodding his head. "Okay. I can agree with that," he smiled, pulling me into the living room with him.

Once we made our way over to the recliner, he sat down and I dropped into his lap. I curled into his chest and his large arms wrapped protectively around me. We sat that way for a while before either of us spoke. Finally, I broke the silence.

"Tell me about yourself, Bray. All I know about you is what happened with you and Andi. Surely there are things about you that they didn't tell me."

"Well, I'm an only child. My mom Connie and I are really close. Dad is always around but seems to be in the background when it comes to the two of us. She went to all of my baseball games in high school and college. As you probably know, I work with the Compton brothers and Andi. I absolutely love what I do there."

I smiled as I learned little tidbits from Bray. It was nice to be conversing with someone other than Andi and Pepper. Ever since I'd met Drake and then after I'd left him, I'd been stuck in a weird world where I worked and spent my free time at home. It was terribly lonely, especially now that the girls had boyfriends.

"What about you, Olive? What's your story?" he asked, kissing the top of my head. Andi and Pepper knew I'd run away from an abusive relationship but didn't know the details. I wasn't sure I'd ever be able to tell anyone the specifics that had made up my time with Drake.

"Well, I always dreamed of leaving Detroit to become a New York model. My highly religious mother hated the idea. When I finally got the guts to do it, she disowned me for it. I came to the city with a bag full of clothes and a small amount of cash, but my heart was completely in it. Things weren't looking up until I met a well-known photographer named Drake. We hit it off right away. It wasn't until after I moved in with him that I learned he was abusive," I admitted, allowing a tear to roll down my face and wet his shirt.

"Abusive how?" he asked quietly. His body was tense, like it was ready to snap into action.

"The specifics are better left unsaid. He crossed the line one night and I managed to escape. That next day, I found Andi and they took me in. A complete stranger. Her heart was so big, and she did it without a moment's hesitation. Now you see why I owe her everything and would die before I hurt her. This thing between us complicates and confuses everything. And on top of feeling guilty about Andi, I feel dumbfounded as to how you just waltzed in here and squashed my fears with just one look. It really isn't fair—the one moment I finally feel safe is one I can't revel in."

He squeezed me to him, and I allowed myself this temporary moment of happiness.

"Andi is a great, loving person. That's why I think she would be okay with your dating me. I think you've made it to be something worse in your head than it actually is. And it makes me so fucking glad that I make you feel safe—you deserve to feel that way. Do you not ever run into him with your modeling jobs?" he asked, bringing the subject back to Drake.

"Since we were together for so long, I knew which types of jobs he took and who he worked with. I'm really careful to avoid where I might run into him. To be quite honest, if I ever see him again, it could be very bad for me," I confided, a shiver coursing through me.

"Why? How could it be very bad for you?" he asked, alarmed, and sat up.

Turning to look at him, I tried to quell the fear as my thoughts considered what Drake would do based upon the horrors he'd already done to me. "I don't know, but I think, given the chance, he would kill me," I told him honestly.

"What the fuck?" he roared, nearly knocking me into the floor.

I jumped at his sudden tone, and my heart raced.

36

"I'm sorry. I didn't mean to scare you, but shit, that's quite a bomb you just dropped on me. What the fuck did this asshole do to you that you would fear for your life? What's his last name? I'll teach him to pick on women," he growled angrily.

"Bray, it's fine. I avoid going out because I don't want to run into him anywhere. That's why Andi had her party here. I'm completely socially inept. Last time I went out with Andi and Jackson, I nearly had a panic attack when Jackson's friend Ian hit on me," I sighed.

"Olive, I don't care where we go. This is the first time I've been able to enjoy myself since the breakup with Andi. I've been coasting along, pissed off at the world and myself. Now that I've met you, I actually have been able to think of something else and it feels fucking great."

I looked over at him and smiled. His blue eyes twinkled as he grinned back at me. The guy truly was a heartthrob.

"So tell me about what happened with Andi. Why would you cheat on a great girl like her?" I questioned, really needing to know the answer.

He groaned and bowed his head. "Olive, I truly messed up. Andi is a great girl. We would have been better off as friends. She was naïve and came from an unloving family. I was completely taken with her and wanted to protect her. We loved each other, but eventually the spark began to fade. When school got intense towards the end, we spent less and less time together.

"One day, a girl from one of my classes came to see my roommate. She threw herself at me and I stupidly allowed it to progress. Andi walked in on us and I was horrified at myself. Had I not been a stupid man, I would have told her we needed to spend some time apart instead of cheating on her. The cheating blindsided her and she took it really hard.

"Believe me, I begged and begged her to come back to me. Mostly it was because I saw how it completely crushed her. I just wanted to fix her. Dammit, Olive, she totally lost it because of me."

Looking into his eyes, I could see the guilt. People made mistakes, and unfortunately for Bray, he got to relive them every day now that he worked with Andi. Pepper didn't have any problems with reminding him about those mistakes either.

"Bray, it was a mistake and you feel badly about it. I think it's time you start to move on from it. I sure as heck would love to forget my past."

"Sounds like a plan. Now, to completely change the subject, I just want to tell you that your little obsession with tiny shorts is fucking hot," he declared, sliding his hand across the back of my thigh just under my shorts.

"Glad you approve," I teased.

"Actually, I don't approve of them at all. I think you need to take them off. *Now*."

Chapter SEVEN

Bray

OLIVE GIGGLED AT my suggestion to take her shorts off. Being with her like this felt so right. It was nice sitting with her, getting things I'd never been able to talk to anyone about before off my chest.

"I found her, you know," I confessed sadly.

Olive turned her head to look at me again. Her lips parted slightly at the sudden change of my voice. She pecked me on the cheek, urging me to go on.

"After graduation, when stupid Steph came up and hugged me, Andi thought I hadn't really changed. That night, she went to her dorm and proceeded to take all of her antidepressants with alcohol." I paused, choking back the bile that had risen in my throat at the memory of seeing her that night.

Olive's eyes wildly searched mine, waiting for the rest of the story.

"Anyway, God, this part is awful. I got a call from her and she was slurring, completely incoherent," I sighed as tears burned my eyes. "She was fucking lifeless. I shook her but she was entirely out of it. Her eyes were rolled back and she was drooling. But the part I will never be able to erase from my mind were her lips. They were so fucking blue."

Olive was quietly sobbing as I described that night. I finally let a tear escape and hastily wiped it away.

"She was barely breathing and she was fucking cold," I growled, shaking my head at the vision.

Olive slipped her arms around me and squeezed.

"Once I realized she had overdosed, I shoved my fingers down her throat. All that mattered was getting the pills out of her and quickly. She vomited all over the both of us. I didn't care. Olive, all I cared about was that she made it out alive. From that point on, I backed away. Andi was better off without me in her life. The fact that I was the cause of her nearly ending her life was almost too much to bear. As much as I hate Jackson, I'm glad she has him." I sighed as I rehashed those memories and the Chinese food fought wildly in my stomach to make a reappearance.

Olive studied me for a few minutes before standing to go into the kitchen. When she walked back out with a tub of ice cream, two spoons, and an ornery grin, I couldn't help but smile back at her.

"Enough with the depressing topics. We have a date with American Idol," she declared. She motioned to her room and I stood to follow her in there. Either she swayed her hips as a natural way of walking or she did it to tease me—regardless, it was hot as hell.

After she put on the show and I'd slipped off my shoes to get more comfortable, we sat together in the bed eating ice cream. I couldn't care less about the show, but watching her get so into it was entertaining in and of itself.

"Who do you want to win?" she asked excitedly during a commercial break. We'd finished off the ice cream and she set it on the table next to the bed.

"Uh, Jennifer Lopez?" I answered, having no idea what to say. She was the only one I recognized from the show.

"What? Bray! She's a judge, dork. You weren't paying attention at all," she said, pretending to be annoyed.

Laughing at her, I poked her in the ribs, making her squeal. "I was paying attention, just not to the show," I teased, wagging my eyebrows at her.

She playfully punched me in the belly. Sitting up, I grabbed her hips and pulled her down the bed off the pillows.

"Just for that, you're getting tickled. No mercy now," I growled, making her shriek with laughter. Grabbing both hands, I held them easily with one of my hands and straddled her, pinning her to the bed. Using my free hand, I tickled her ribs some more. She screamed and thrashed wildly underneath me.

"Stop it, you big jerk, or else!" she threatened between laughing gasps. I pulled my hand away, giving her a moment to catch her breath.

"Or else what?" I demanded, wriggling my fingers just over her ribs again. She squirmed to get away but was unsuccessful. Her tiny frame was no match for my massive one.

"Or else I'll kick you out," she huffed.

Laughing at her, I took my fingers and gently dragged them down the side of her ribs instead of tickling her. Her eyes flew to mine, and once she realized they were now filled with desire, she relaxed under me. Leaning over with her hands still pinned, I gently sucked her neck. As I suckled her soft skin, she panted underneath me.

My kisses moved down to the skin that was accessible above her tank top and she exhaled heavily. Using my teeth, I pulled part of her shirt down, exposing one breast. She inhaled sharply when I dragged my tongue along her flesh just above her nipple. Finally, I released her hands so I could pull the tank down farther, revealing both of her perky mounds.

Her hands found my hair, latching on as I fully sucked a nipple into my mouth.

"Bray," she moaned as I gently brought it between my teeth, teasing it with a small nip. She reached over for the lamp and switched it off before I could argue. Luckily, the light from the television allowed me to still see her perfect body.

Sitting up, I yanked off my shirt and tossed it off the bed. Leaning back over her, I found her lips again with mine and we kissed, unrushed. Her fingers trailed a pattern along my back almost as if she were memorizing the contours of my skin.

While kissing, I grabbed a breast with my hand, tweaking her nipple with my thumb. Eventually, my hand slid across her tank and over her stomach to the area between her legs that was most likely throbbing for me. Slipping my hand under the waistband of her tiny shorts, I found where she was wet for me and slid my finger in.

As I stroked her, quickly locating her g-spot, she started raising her hips to meet my movements. Hastily, she pulled down her shorts to give me better access. Chuckling into her mouth, I pulled away to look at her. The light from the television created shadows that danced across her face but did little to hide the desire that was painted there.

I sat up on my knees and finished pulling her shorts, along with her panties, the rest of the way off. She spread her legs and I slipped in another finger, picking my pace back up. Her breaths were coming on quickly as she got close to her orgasm. Wanting to see her completely naked, I reached for the bottom of her tank to pull it off but her hand swatted it away.

Confused, I looked up at her quizzically and was met with a devastated look.

"Shit. What's wrong, Olive?" I asked, worry lacing my voice. Pulling my fingers from her, I sat up on my knees, looking down at her. She chewed on her lip and tears welled in her eyes, threatening to spill over.

Lying down beside her on my elbow, I put my hand on her

cheek to turn her towards me. Whatever was going on with her, I was going to figure it out right now.

"Olive. Tell me," I commanded gently.

Her eyes darted away from mine and a tear escaped. She batted it away and sighed in frustration. "He marred me," she barely whispered.

I could feel my entire body tense up, and my heart raced. My hand fell to her tank and gently stroked across her belly over her shirt.

"Here?" I asked, looking up at her.

She nodded as shame crossed over her face. Fucking shame for what that asshole had done to her.

"I'll kill him," I promised, no hint of humor in my voice.

"Not if he kills me first," she spoke sadly. My hand that was splayed across her midsection angrily fisted her shirt. She flinched and I immediately released her shirt.

"Please show me," I urged, trying to control the rage towards that dickhead in my voice.

Leaning over, she turned the lamp back on. Lying back down, she sighed heavily as she slowly started inching her shirt up.

Pausing with the shirt she says, "It's disgusting. I'm ashamed for you to see this part of me."

"Olive, you'll never be disgusting to me. Now show me or I'll be forced to rip your shirt off and I promise I'll enjoy every second doing it," I told her suggestively, hoping to lighten her mood. Her frown turned into a hopeful smile that was absolutely stunning.

Dropping my head, I kissed her pubic bone. Inching up a bit, I kissed a little higher. Slowly, she raised her shirt little by little as I kissed what felt like scarred skin. When I made it to her belly button, I dipped my tongue inside and she whimpered in pleasure. Not lingering there, I continued my trail of kisses up her belly until she'd lifted her shirt up over her breasts.

Finally, I looked into her eyes, waiting for permission. She chewed her lip nervously but nodded.

Chapter EIGHT

Olive

I COULDN'T BELIEVE I was willingly about to show Bray something that nobody but the doctor and nurse had seen before. Even Pepper and Andi were excluded from seeing my mutilated torso. Once I nodded, Bray sat up. His eyes, which had shone with contentment, quickly morphed into anger once they skittered over my body.

Time stood still as I watched his jaw click furiously and his teeth ground against each other. The muscles in his neck had tightened unnaturally, and his vein stood out prominently. His lips were pursed together in a grim line. Eventually, his eyes met mine again. The anger left them and compassion filled them.

"Olive, I'm so sorry," he whispered almost inaudibly. Bowing his head, he kissed along each scar, paying attention to every one of them. It was incredibly intimate. For just having met, we were crazily drawn to each other as if our spirits were tethered.

When he finished his methodical kissing, he crawled up beside me and rubbed my belly.

"Don't ever hide your scars from me. I'll think you're beautiful no matter what," he promised and my heart soared. It was ridiculous how fast I was latching on to Bray. Hiding it from Andi was going to be nearly impossible. I wanted to shout to the world that this beautiful, gentle, sweet man was mine.

Pulling my shirt completely off, I leaned over and kissed him tentatively on the lips. He unfastened his jeans and wriggled out of them, eventually kicking them off the bed. Producing a condom that must have come from his pants, he tore it open and slid it on his length. Rolling onto his back, he pulled me on top of him.

"I want to see all of you," he declared, eyes smoldering.

Nodding, I straddled him and slid down over his massive cock. Grabbing both hips with his hands, he guided me up and down on his shaft. This was a position Drake had never allowed, and it was quickly becoming my favorite.

"You're so damn sexy," he growled as I felt my orgasm getting closer. With each bounce, I felt deliciously stretched. Electric pulses shot through me as my body prepared to come. My hands slid up his chest and grabbed a fistful of flesh when I came wildly. I moaned when I felt him pump his own orgasm into me.

I curled up on his chest and sighed. "Bray, this feels so good being with you this way. I can't help but feel sad though that we're hidden in our little bubble. We can't stay in here forever, and we have to be careful with this relationship.

"Olive, let's tell them tomorrow," he suggested, but I frowned. I had to figure out how I was going to begin to explain the situation that was me and Bray to the girls.

"I promise I'll tell them eventually. Let me figure out the best way to do that," I expressed to him. Sliding off of him, I climbed off my bed and headed to the dresser. Grabbing a scarf that was draped over the mirror, I wrapped my hair carefully. "Ready for a shower?" I asked saucily as I sashayed into the bathroom.

The sound of the bedsprings and heavy footsteps behind me had me grinning the whole way there.

We hardly slept last night as we spent our time getting to know each other in every possible way. When Bray's phone alarm went off this morning, he reluctantly left to go to work but not before putting our numbers in each other's phones.

I didn't have any modeling gigs today so I attempted to call my mother. She never took my calls, but I hoped I might get her to talk to me eventually. Dialing her number, she picked up on the second ring.

"Hello?" Her tone was sweet which meant she obviously had not taken the time to look at the caller ID.

"Momma?" I asked hesitantly, afraid she would hang up on me.

"What do you want, child?" she asked, voice quickly cooling. At least she was speaking to me.

"Momma, I miss you. Have you been getting the money I've been sending to you? How's Opal?" I asked in a rush, eager to get some answers.

She sighed but didn't hang up. Progress.

"Yes, I got the devil's money. I'm not spending a dime of it. If you'll please tell me your address, I'll mail the checks back to you. And Opal... I can't even talk to you about her right now," she clipped out. Opal was my beautiful younger sister, who would be eighteen this month. We'd been so close until my mother had refused to allow me to be a part of their lives.

"Momma, please just use the money. You and Opal need it more than I do. I was thinking maybe I could come see you for Christmas," I said hopefully. I'd only been able to recently start sending Momma checks. While with Drake, he'd controlled every dime.

"I will make do. The church provides when times are tight. I believe I'll be busy for Christmas," she replied snootily.

My heart sank. I missed her and my little sister. For an entire year, I'd been trying to contact them, and only recently had I been able to get her to actually answer the phone. This was the most she'd ever spoken to me in over a year. I needed to tread lightly if I wanted to continue our conversation.

"Um, okay. Well, maybe another time?" I questioned. She sighed loudly into the phone and I cringed.

"We'll see, Olive. Is that all you called about? Because I need to get back to working on the church bulletin. They don't pay me to lollygag. Say hello to your harlot sister," she spat out at me.

"What?" I started to ask but was cut off by the dial tone. Tears filled my eyes, but I blinked them away. What had she meant by her last comment? Was Opal here in New York City?

Walking over to the window, I watched the people like I would any other day while at home and not working. They all bustled along in a hurry to get to their jobs and appointments. I watched them with envy as they went on with their lives without a worry in the world.

My life was far from normal. I had a horrible relationship with my mother. I was betraying my best friend by sleeping with her ex-fiancé. And I couldn't go out in public like a normal person in fear of getting stalked by my abusive ex. Those people down below just hustled by without a care in the world.

I sighed in frustration and set to cleaning the apartment. If there was one thing I could control, it was the cleanliness of where I lived.

A couple of hours later, I showed up at my weekly appointment. Ever since Drake had hurt me so badly, I'd taken up two new hobbies—going to the indoor firing range and self-defense classes. If I had learned anything from him, it was that if I ever saw him again, I would need to know how to both shoot a gun and defend myself. He would want to finish what he'd started. Too bad for him, I had no intentions of letting him.

When I pulled open the door, all earlier frustration from the conversation with my mother faded away. When I was here, I was able to block everything else and focus on one thing. *My target.*

"Hey, Princess Tiana," Jo's gravelly voice called out from across the counter. I grinned at her. Jo wasn't much taller than the counter, but she was a ball full of fire. She was the owner of the range and didn't take crap from anyone. Thankfully for me, she'd seen it upon herself to take me under her wing and show me the ropes.

"Hey, Momma Jo," I said and sat my purse up on the counter. She slid the paperwork over to me as I handed over my license.

"You're looking especially happy today. What gives?" she asked as she typed in the information from my driver's license into the computer. I scrawled my signature on the form and slid it over to her along with my money for the range fees.

Sighing, I couldn't help the cheesy grin that spread over my face. "I met someone."

Even though I never told Jo why I'd started practicing two months ago, she knew deep down. I could tell. It made me wonder if, once upon a time, she too had dealt with an abusive person in the past. There was just something about her that made me think that. Of course I would never ask.

"And who is this 'someone'? Is he a good guy?" she questioned, turning to me. Her eyebrows were raised in both question and concern.

"He's great, actually," I admitted, leaving out the part where he's pretty much forbidden.

She must have sensed that I was hiding something because she frowned. "Tell him he better treat you well or Jo will hunt him down," she grumbled before heading over to the cabinet to retrieve my gun. Technically it wasn't my gun yet since it was on layaway, but it would be my gun soon. She efficiently pulled out the small Glock 19. I'd fallen in love with this gun because it was smaller and easier to handle. Two more payments and it would be mine.

While she gathered the ammunition, safety glasses, and ear protection, I walked over to the lockers and stuffed my purse and coat inside. After retrieving the gun and equipment, I headed into designated firing area and stepped into the first booth. Nobody was in at the moment, and I sighed happily. I preferred being here alone, which was why I'd chosen the middle of the week during the workday to do my target practice.

Once my ear protection was in place and safety glasses were on, I loaded the gun and took the safety off. Spreading my legs slightly, I raised my arms and aimed at the target. With slight squeezes, I shot off all the rounds in rapid succession, making a nice holey pattern in the center of my target's head.

Chapter NINE

Bray

"HEY, JACKSON, CAN you come here and take a look at something for a second?" I asked, poking my head into his office. He looked mildly shocked that I was asking for his help but recovered as his usual smirk replaced it.

Following me back into my office, I motioned for him to take a look at my computer. Realizing it was truly business related, he became serious.

"What's this?" he asked, pointing at my screen.

"I have this design I've been working on but I want a second pair of eyes on this thing. It's a huge deal and I want to make sure it is something you and Jordan would do."

He reached over, taking the mouse from me, and began clicking through my work. I could tell he was running through it with a fine-tooth comb, looking for anything to nitpick at me about. Fortunately, I didn't care. This job was too big to worry about egos. I needed experience to double-check it.

"Bray, honestly, I'm quite amazed. Normally, we probably wouldn't have taken on that job. Those dimensions are nearly impossible to work with. You've managed to make the design very functional. That's exactly what I would do. Great job," he said, slapping me on the shoulder.

I hadn't been expecting such a positive reaction from him. From Jordan, yes, but never from Jackson.

"Uh, thanks. I'll set up a meeting with him and let him know it's done. I appreciate your help, man," I said honestly. He nodded and left my office.

I was busy working when I got a call. After rolling my eyes because I'd expected my mother, I grinned once I realized it was actually Olive.

"Hey," I smiled into the phone when I answered.

"Hey yourself," she teased. Her voice was sweet as honey, and I couldn't wait to see her again.

"What are you doing tonight?" I questioned.

"I didn't have any plans but Andi mentioned something about staying in and watching a movie. I guess Jackson has to go help his mom or something," she said, pouting. I smiled as I imagined her plump bottom lip poking out.

"Damn. I really wanted to see you. Maybe I could sneak in after she goes to bed," I suggested.

"That sounds like a really good idea, Bray," she said cheerfully. "I already miss our long talks."

"I'll talk to you soon, Ollie," I teased. Her silence told me that I'd said something wrong.

She gulped loudly into the phone. "Um, yeah, okay," she said quietly before hanging up, leaving me to wonder exactly what it was I'd said.

"I'm so glad you asked me to dinner, Bray. I feel like we never see each other anymore," Mom said as she sipped her wine.

"Yeah, I'm sorry, Mom. Ever since I started this new job, things have been crazy busy. They're a bigger firm than my old place, so I'm expected to do bigger projects. I love it but they definitely keep me busy," I told her, taking a bite of my pasta primavera.

"Sweetie, I'm proud of you. You worked so hard in college for this. Your dreams are finally coming true. How was Andi's party the other night?" she asked, nibbling on her bread.

I grinned like a fool. "Thanks, Mom. It was great. I actually met someone that I really like."

"Bray, that's wonderful! I'm so excited for you. Please tell me about this gal," she chirped happily, no longer interested in her dinner. "She must be something special to catch your interest."

"Well, she's tall and beautiful. Her name is Olive and she models here in New York. The only problem is that she's Andi's roommate," I sighed.

She narrowed her eyes as she mulled over what I was saying. "And what does Andi think about this?" she clipped out pointedly. This conversation wasn't going exactly like I'd planned.

"She doesn't know," I admitted. "We're keeping it from her until we can figure out a way to best tell her." It made us seem like the biggest fucking assholes on the planet.

"Hmmm," she said, picking at her bread. Her response said it all. She didn't approve. Not a good way to start things off.

"Mom, it's not what you think. Olive just doesn't want to hurt Andi. Neither do I, for that matter. We're going to tell her and she'll probably be just fine with it."

"Well, son, I suppose Andi broke up with you in the first place. She doesn't really have much room to get upset by whom you date," she said, still seemingly unconvinced.

"Uh, yeah, about that…"

She frowned when she saw the guilty look on my face.

"Mom, I need to tell you something. Andi and I broke up because I cheated on her," I confessed shamefully.

53

Her face morphed into a glare and she dropped her fork with a clatter. "You *what?*" she asked shrilly. The look she gave me was one of both anger and disappointment.

"Things with Andi had become routine. When a girl came on to me, I just went with it. She caught us, Mom. In the fucking act," I grumbled, palming my face.

"Language, mister," she huffed.

Refraining from rolling my eyes, I continued. "Mom, she took it so fuc-freaking hard. I begged her to take me back. She was a shell of herself because of me. At graduation, I really thought we might get back together, but when that girl hugged me, Andi lost her mind. For some reason, she thought it would be a good idea to take all of her antidepressants," I confessed, no longer hungry. Her horrified expression filled me again with guilt.

"Brayden Edward Greene, of all things. I'm stunned. I don't even know what to say right now."

"Mom, don't say anything. Just let me finish. I found her and intercepted the almost overdose. She was taken to the hospital, where they pumped her stomach. I nearly ruined her life. Andi almost died because of me."

It was nice to finally get it off my chest to my mother. She hadn't known the whole story, and the look on her face made me realize why I'd waited so long to tell her. It was full of disgust. My heart sank.

"That poor girl," she said simply as she fought back tears.

"Yes, I know. And I feel bad about it. Thankfully, we're able to be friends again. Her shrink says it would be good for her to embrace a friendship with me since we are forced to work to-gether."

"Shrink?" she asked numbly.

"Yes. She sees a shrink because of me. Anyway, I met her roommate Olive and she's absolutely amazing. We have a strong connec—" I start to say, but she cut me off by waving a hand in my face.

"Stop right there. Whatever it is you're doing with this Olive girl needs to stop. Obviously Andi is far too fragile to withstand any more hurt from you, Brayden. This little fling with Olive will further inflict pain on poor Andi. My mind is still reeling at what you did to her. You're my son but I'm angry. Angry at what you did and angry that you waited nearly six months to tell me about it. I feel foolish at thinking it was her fault this entire time."

"I know, and I'm sorry, Mom. But what Olive and I have isn't a little fling. She understands me and I get her too. We were just dealt an unfortunate hand that she my ex's best friend."

"Brayden, I want you to listen to me. Break it off now. You've only seen her for what, two days now? I think you can easily back out of what you're doing before either of you gets hurt. I'm telling you, if you honestly believe that Andi will be okay with this, then you're not using your brain. She will be ab-solutely crushed. The poor girl doesn't need any more nonsense from you. If this Olive girl really cares about her, she'll agree and step away from whatever it is you two are doing. Andi is more important than your casual fuck," she said snippily.

My mouth gaped at my mother's use of the word "fuck." She was definitely pissed because she never cursed.

"Mom, Olive isn't a casual fuck!" I exclaimed, attempting to make her understand the situation.

"Brayden, do not raise your voice at me. Now this is the end of this discussion. If you'll excuse me, I must get going. Thank you for dinner. Do the right thing, honey," she advised as she snatched up her purse and stalked out of the restaurant.

Chapter TEN

Olive

"WHAT DO YOU want to watch? Romantic comedy or drama?" Andi asked, holding up two movies.

"Definitely the romantic comedy," I decided as I crawled into her bed. She had the biggest television, and typically the three of us girls would cram onto her bed to watch movies.

"You okay, Olive? You seem like your head's somewhere else," she observed as she scrutinized me.

I sat up nervously and tried to mask the guilty look that undoubtedly was shining on my face like a beacon. "I'm fine. Everything's fine," I squeaked out.

She narrowed her eyes but decided to let it go. After putting the movie in, she sat beside me with the popcorn in her lap.

"You don't always have to guard what you're thinking, hon. Jackson does the same fucking thing, and in the end, it just causes more stress for him. If you ever want to talk about what happened with Drake or whatever is bothering you now, you know I'll be there. You're one of my best friends. I will always be there for you."

Tears filled my eyes but I quickly blinked them back and gave her a smile. In that moment, I should have told her, but I was afraid to. The guilt was so overwhelming that I felt nauseated.

"I sure hope so, Andi. You know I love you dearly too."

She gave me a quick hug and we settled back against the pillows as the movie began.

We were soon giggling through the movie when we heard voices and a door slam shut. It sounded like Jordan and Pepper were having a fight. I frowned and looked over at Andi when suddenly the bedroom door flung open and a dark-haired man stepped into the room, glaring at us.

We both gasped upon realizing that he had a gun aimed at us. Andi's hand reached for mine and squeezed. The wild look in his eyes reminded me of Drake, and I shuddered.

"Get up, both of you," he snarled at us. We scrambled from the bed, still holding hands, and hesitantly walked over to him. Yanking Andi by the arm, he dragged her through the door and down the hallway to Pepper's bedroom door.

"Get her out of there," he ordered to me. My eyes darted to Andi, who was glaring at him, but I obeyed since the gun was trained on her.

"Pepper?" I asked nervously through the door.

"Don't fucking open the door!" Andi shrieked from beside me.

The crazed man lunged at her. I was momentarily stunned when he hit her across the head with his pistol and she went down with a thud. He turned his glare to me and I burst into tears.

"Open the door, Peppermint Pussy, or your girlfriends are going to each take a bullet in the head," he spat, putting the barrel of the gun to my temple. My sobs were uncontrollable. I didn't want Pepper to open the door, but at the same time, I was terrified that this psycho was going to kill us if she didn't.

The door flung open and a very pissed off Pepper glared at him from the threshold. He motioned with a flick of his head for me to go into her room. I ran over to her and grabbed hold of her hand. She squeezed it once for support. We both winced when he dragged Andi into the room by her hair.

My sobs must have intensified because Pepper stepped in front of me, blocking my view of a helpless Andi. Even in this terrifying situation, she was the strong, protective one.

"Cole, just let them go. You can have me. Please just leave them alone," she pleads calmly to him.

Something in him snapped and he stalked over to her. Before she could act, his hand was immediately gripping her throat. "You don't fucking make the rules!" he roared as he choked her.

"Let her go!" I screamed, grabbing at his large arm to try to pull it away from her neck.

"Bitch, you better back off right now or I'll shoot her!" he growled.

I stopped immediately and backed away. One thing I knew from dealing with Drake was that you didn't push an unstable person when they were in a manic state. My tears poured down my face as I stood helplessly watching him with his hands around her neck. He finally released her and I gasped in relief.

Kneeling down, I looked Andi over. She was completely unconscious. We weren't far from the bathroom. If I could find a way to sneak us in there, I could regroup and figure out how to help Pepper. Cole continued to attack Pepper, never dropping his gun. At one point, he twisted her arm painfully behind her back and she screamed. Luckily, she was still holding her own so I started dragging Andi quietly into the bathroom.

Once I got her inside, I softly closed the door and turned the lock.

"Andi, wake up," I whispered urgently to her. She groaned and her eyes fluttered but she remained out of it. I felt her pockets, searching for her cell phone, but came up empty-handed. My own phone sat useless on the nightstand in Andi's room.

When I heard a scream of pain from Pepper, I frantically looked around the bathroom for a weapon. I tried pulling down the shower curtain rod but it was bolted to the wall. He was cussing and they seemed to still be having quite a scuffle, which meant Pepper was keeping him from doing what he really wanted to do.

Searching quickly through the drawers, I found a metal nail file. The sound of a crash made me jump, and I quietly unlocked the door, peeking outside. Jordan had thankfully made it there and was making progress with beating up Cole. Andi moaned and I knelt back down beside her.

"Pepper?" she asked groggily.

"She's out there with that lunatic. Jordan's here though. I'm going to go try to help them. You stay quiet in here," I ordered. She nodded and I stood back up to peek out the bathroom door.

My heart sank when I saw Pepper's lifeless form on the bed. Jordan was pinned under Cole's hulking frame, clearly losing whatever advantage he'd had earlier.

The look on Cole's face made me sick to my stomach. It was the same empty, sadistic look Drake had had on his the night he carved me like a pumpkin. As I watched him punch Jordan, I thought about the many times Drake had punched me. The time he'd kicked me so hard I lost my baby. *My baby.*

Suddenly, I was filled with rage. Seeing the gun on the floor near Cole lit a fire inside me. Bolting from the bathroom, I leapt for the gun and snatched it up. Knowing my shot needed to count, I carefully aimed for the monster's head and fired. For a brief second, I saw Drake with a hole in his head and I smiled, satisfied.

Chapter ELEVEN

Bray

ON THE WAY home, I thought about what Mom had said. Maybe Olive and I weren't thinking about Andi's feelings. Was I naïve to think she'd be okay with it? She'd nearly lost it when I cheated on her. Finding out that her best friend and ex-fiancé were fucking and holding it from her might crush her again. Olive and I really needed to have a talk about this.

My phone rang but I didn't reach it in time before it went to voicemail. Figuring I would check it once I got to my apartment, I didn't worry too much about it. Pulling into my spot, I finally took it from my coat pocket. Olive had called but had not left a voicemail. I dialed her back.

"Bray," she whispered shakily when she answered the phone. The tone of her voice immediately sent me on high alert, making me think she'd had a run-in with Drake.

"What is it Olive?" I questioned anxiously.

"I shot Cole. Bray, I shot someone," she said numbly.

"Olive, you're not making any sense. What the fuck are you talking about?" I demanded, trying to understand what she was trying to say.

She began sobbing, and I backed the car out of the spot so I could drive to her.

"Are you at home?" I asked, trying to keep the panicked sound from my voice.

"No, I'm at the hospital with everyone," she answered sadly. *What in the hell was going on here?*

"Okay, Olive, I'm on my way. Now tell me what happened," I spoke soothingly. I'd already peeled out of my parking garage and was just a few blocks from the hospital.

"Bray, some guy came after Pepper. He tried to rape her. I killed him with his gun. He was a *monster*," she hissed as if she were trying to convince me why she'd done it.

"It's okay, honey. I believe you," I said softly. "Even though I have no idea what you're talking about, I'm sure you were only trying to protect her."

She started crying again as I pulled into the parking garage at the hospital.

"Where are you?" I asked as I found a parking space and shut off the car.

"I'm waiting out in the lobby of the ER," she said, barely a whisper. Jumping from my car, I ran to the elevators and took it to the floor where she was.

Stepping out of the elevator, I saw her sitting in a chair hunched over with her head between her knees and her phone held to her ear. When she looked up and saw me, she turned the phone off and stood up.

Walking quickly, I went up to her and pulled her into my arms. She sobbed uncontrollably and melted into my embrace.

"Shhh. I'm here now," I reassured her. Eventually, she quieted down and sniffled softly.

My mind was racing because I still had no fucking idea what had happened. After a few minutes later, Jordan came walking down the hallway. Walking right up to us, he pulled Olive away from me and hugged her tight.

"Thank you, Olive," he whispered into her hair. She nodded but pulled away to come back over to me.

"What the fuck happened, man?" I asked Jordan. He looked like total shit with his eye almost completely swollen shut.

"Elizabeth—er, 'Pepper' had a crazy stalker that attempted to rape and kill her. Olive shot him in the head," he said almost in disbelief at the last part.

I pulled her close to me and hugged her again. This was too much to take in.

"Okay. Well, um, I think maybe I should take Olive home. She clearly has been through enough. Has she already given her statement to the police?" I asked him.

"Yeah, we're all done with them. We shut the door to Elizabeth's room just avoid it 'til we can get it cleaned up. I think she needs to go home and get some rest. Thanks, Bray, for helping us out."

"Jordan, is everyone okay?" I asked, worried. I was quickly figuring out that Elizabeth was Pepper. Could this night get any more fucking confusing?

"Yeah, man. Andi has a concussion, but she'll be fine. Elizabeth has a broken wrist and was beaten up pretty badly. She'll be okay though," he said, sighing in relief.

"Good to hear. Keep me posted." I slapped him on the back before turning and ushering Olive out to the car.

After we had made it back to the car and I'd helped her in, I got in on my side and sat for a moment trying to figure out how she was feeling. Olive was clearly in shock. She rotated between crying and having a glazed-over look to her eyes.

"Olive, are you going to be okay? Do you want to talk about it?" I asked her.

She turned to me with a vacant look in her eyes. "I'll be fine—just tired. I still can't believe I shot him," she said.

Reaching over, I grabbed her hand and squeezed it. The drive home was quiet as she stared blankly out the window, clearly lost in her thoughts. We didn't speak again until we were back in the apartment.

"Why don't you grab a hot shower and I'll fix you something to eat," I suggested. Nodding her head, she walked towards her room while I went to the kitchen.

I rummaged in the cabinets and found a can of chicken noodle soup. Once I had heated it up and located some crackers, she re-surfaced fresh-faced and smelling like soap. When she passed me to go to the table, I couldn't help but grin when I noticed her really short red shorts that barely covered her ass.

"Here. Hope you like this," I told her, setting the bowl down in front of her.

She nodded and smiled for the first time tonight. "Thanks, Bray. You're a sweet guy," she said as she ate. Something had shifted in the air, and the tone had felt dismissive. "You can go on home. I'll be fine," she sighed, not looking up at me.

Yes, definitely dismissive.

"Olive, I'll sleep on the couch, but I think you'll feel better if someone stays with you tonight. Okay?"

"Bray, I don't need a babysitter. I'm not hurt," she said icily as her eyes met mine with a glare. Olive was definitely in shock. This was uncharacteristic for her.

"Well, you'll just have to be pissed at me because I'm not leaving. End of discussion," I said, meeting her gaze with equal intensity. There was no chance in the world I would leave her like this.

"Whatever," she spat as she dropped her spoon in the bowl and stood up quickly. Not looking in my direction, she strolled past me and slammed the door to her room once inside.

"Fuck," I muttered under my breath as I cleaned up the dishes. Grabbing a blanket from the basket near the end of the couch, I settled on the sofa for the night.

Chapter TWELVE

Olive

I SHOT SOMEONE. I freaking shot someone. My mind still reeled at the memory of raising the gun and shooting Cole in the forehead. I had a feeling a day wouldn't go by where I wouldn't think about that moment when I'd taken someone's life.

If my mother knew about this, she'd certainly disown me for good. Modeling in the Big Apple was small stuff compared to murder. Even though I'd done it to stop Cole from hurting Jordan and Pepper more than he already had, I still felt horrible about it.

The entire night, I tossed and turned as I rehashed that scene both consciously and while asleep. During one dream, I kept seeing the blood splatter behind him in slow motion over and over as if it were on replay. I woke with a start, feeling instantly nauseated. Jumping from the bed, I bolted to my bathroom and barely made it before I emptied the contents of my stomach into the toilet.

Heavy footsteps came up behind me, and I shuddered when large hands gathered my hair. Realizing that Bray was still here and helping me even though I'd been completely nasty to him earlier, I felt tears sting my eyes.

When I stopped dry heaving, he stepped away from me, and

I heard the faucet turn on. Moments later, a cool rag went over the back of my neck.

He must have located a hair tie because soon after he was pulling my hair into a ponytail. This guy was amazing. Too bad we were over before we had even begun. Without speaking, he comforted me by gently rubbing my back as I hugged the toilet seat.

Everything had come into perspective for me today after I'd shot Cole. I'd nearly lost my two best friends tonight. Whatever it was that Bray and I had started needed to stop. I loved Andi like a sister and could never hurt her. Having been put in the position we were in, I quickly realized that our friendship needed to come first and foremost. I barely knew Bray and couldn't jeopardize me and Andi over our fling.

Even though I told myself it was a fling, I knew better. Had he been any other guy, besides my best friend's ex, I knew we could have a future together. My luck with guys was just total crap. I was better off not dating anyone at all. Clearly I had the worst choice in men.

"Come on. Let's get you back to bed," he said, voice still gravelly from sleep. Shakily, I stood up and swayed a bit. His hands instantly grabbed my hips to steady me and my body reacted with a shiver. I was supposed to be avoiding him, not secretly wishing he would make love to me.

Once we made it to the bed, he helped me get back under the covers. He looked so hot with his wrinkly shirt and messy hair. I felt like such a hateful person to push him away like I had.

"Stay with me," I whispered before I could stop the words from slipping out.

Nodding, he pulled off his shirt but left on his jeans and crawled under the covers with me. His giant arm wrapped protectively around me and he pulled me close to him. In his arms, I felt safe and fell asleep quickly. The nightmares stayed away for the rest of the night.

"Here you go," I said, smiling at Pepper as I handed her a cup of hot tea. She looked absolutely horrible, and for some reason, I felt better about Cole's demise yesterday after seeing her.

"You guys are smothering me," she teased but squeezed my hand when I sat down next to her.

"That's what friends are for," Andi joked back.

The guys were boxing up Pepper's things while we sat on the couch and watched. Every so often, Pepper would hoarsely bark orders at them. It was good to see she was still her old self.

"I can't believe you're leaving us," I said sadly, looking over at her.

"Oh, come on. I'll see you guys all the time," she confirmed, voice raspy.

Andi asked her a question, and I took that moment to look over at Bray as he walked by with a box. His eyes were on mine the entire time as he strode past.

Things last night had been strange and even weirder this morning. I'd let him comfort me, but we hadn't kissed or touched other than hugging. This morning, he had run out to grab us some coffee and donuts. He'd come back with everyone else. Thankfully, Andi and Pepper still hadn't realized what had happened with us.

"What do you think?" Andi asked, dragging me from my thoughts. I hadn't really been listening, so I looked at her dumbly. She looked sad, probably assuming I was still in shock over Cole when in actuality I was thinking about her ex-fiancé. My stomach churned with guilt.

"Um, what were you guys saying?" I questioned, having been caught not paying attention.

"We were thinking of ordering a couple of pizzas. Does that sound okay?"

"Oh, yes, sure. I'm sure Bray will be fine with that too," I said quickly.

The confused look on her face made me cringe at my words. *Crap!*

"I mean, uh, all of the guys probably would like some pizza," I stuttered, trying to backtrack over my previous words.

Pepper and Andi studied me for a moment. I could see the wheels turning in both of their heads and I wanted to run from the room.

"I'll eat whatever," I declared briefly and stood up. "I'm going to go see if Jackson and Jordan need any help." The girls exchanged glances before Andi grabbed her phone to order the pizza. I was failing miserably at keeping this from them. It was a good thing I'd decided to stop my rendezvous with Bray before it progressed any further.

When Bray walked back into Pepper's bedroom, where I was now tossing the contents of her sock drawer into a basket, he glanced over at me. Our eyes met and I could see the questions in them but I looked away. I was sure he was hurt but we had to stop. I hoped I could talk to him about my decision later today.

Bray continued to try and meet my gaze for the rest of the afternoon while we worked. As we ate pizza, he practically stared at me the entire time. Finally, I looked at him with a 'what do you want' glare. He frowned and shook his head at me.

"Okay, guys. I think I'm going to head home for the night since we're about finished here. If you need help tomorrow, just give me a call," he said and stalked out of the kitchen.

Everyone waved their goodbyes while I just stared at him as he walked out. Tears welled in my eyes and I excused myself, running to my room, where I barely made it before I started sobbing.

Chapter
THIRTEEN

Bray

I'D THOUGHT OLIVE was just in shock yesterday, but it was clear by her behavior today that she didn't have any desire to want to be with me anymore. Looked like Mom had gotten her wish. Instead of going home, I went straight to the gym.

After several hours of pouring my anger into my workout, I finally went home, mentally and physically exhausted. Once home, I took a quick shower. Later, I realized I had a missed call from Olive, who had left a voicemail. Pressing the play button, I tensed at what she was going to say.

"Bray, look, I'm sorry if I led you on but we can't be together anymore. I can't hurt Andi like that. Take care."

Take fucking care? Slamming down the phone on the bed, I pulled my laptop from the bedside table. After it powered on, I searched for photographers in the modeling scene in New York. There were thousands. I narrowed my search, looking for Drake. Even though Olive was blowing me off, I still wanted to know more about that asshole.

Coming across only one named Drake, I pulled up the webpage. A grinning, dark-skinned man in an expensive shirt filled my screen. His smile couldn't mask the evil that was so clearly painted in his eyes. To most people, he would seem like a normal guy. Since I knew what he had done to Olive, I saw right past his façade.

I took a screenshot of the page and emailed it to myself at work. Olive might not want to see me anymore, but I would still do what I could to look out for her. Her fear of running into him was real, and there was no way I could sit back and ignore that.

Thinking about her stomach, I felt furious once again. The night she'd showed me her scars, I'd wanted to punch a hole through the fucking headboard. That asshole had carved "Property of Drake" across her entire abdomen. He'd mutilated her, and I wanted to kill him for it. Briefly, I wondered how many other women he'd hurt, and it took everything in me not to throw my laptop across the room. Needing to cool off, I texted Olive.

Me: I got your message. Even though I don't like it, I get what you're saying. Let's at least be friends. We've confided so much in each other already. Please don't shut me out completely.

I hoped she would at least let us be friends. As hard as it would be to not kiss and touch her, it would be better than not seeing her at all. Moments later, my phone chimed.

Olive: Friends sounds good but promise me you won't try to take things further. I have a hard time telling you no. If you care about me, you won't push it.

Groaning, I typed out my response, knowing it would be difficult to do what she'd asked.

Me: I will try my hardest. How are you doing tonight?

Olive: Fine. It feels weird without Pepper's things here. Since Andi is with Jackson and Pepper is gone now, it feels incredibly lonely here.

Me: Do you want me to come over?

Olive: No.

Me: Okay, okay. What about breakfast in the morning? I could bring bagels and coffee.

Olive: Is this a "friendly" breakfast?
Me: The friendliest. See you in the morning.

For someone who'd suggested we remain friends, she was killing me in those tiny white shorts with the word "pink" scrawled across her cute little ass. I followed her into the kitchen and set down our breakfast.

"How are you doing this morning?" I asked, looking up at her.

She smiled genuinely at me. "I'm doing just fine, Bray. You don't have to babysit me," she teased. It was hard to not pull her to me and kiss her plump lips. When she caught me staring at them, she chewed on the bottom one.

"Shit. Sorry, Olive. How are Andi and Pepper doing?" I questioned.

"I texted Andi earlier and she's back to her normal self. Pepper called me right before you came over. Her wrist still hurts but she's got good pain medicine so she'll be all right."

"When's your next modeling job?" I asked, wondering about her work schedule.

She frowned and sipped her coffee. "Things are slow right now. I have a couple in the coming few weeks, but nothing this week or next."

"So you'll be in this apartment alone for two weeks?" I asked incredulously.

Her bottom lip pouted out as she slowly nodded her head.

"Fuck that. I'll come over every day. You're not sitting here by yourself," I said sternly. She sighed but didn't argue, which told me she really was lonely.

"Fine, Bray, but we should go to the market today. We can't have takeout every day, and you eat a lot," she joked, poking me in the side.

I jumped away, laughing. "Do that again and I'll hold you down like the other night. I won't have mercy on you on this time," I chuckled.

She attempted to glare evilly at me, but when I reached for her, she squealed, jerking away from me.

"That's what I thought," I said smugly as I spread some cream cheese on my bagel. Taking a bite, I looked over at her. The way she was watching me as I ate wasn't innocent in the least bit. But a promise was a promise. "What?" I questioned.

Her tongue darted out, licking her bottom lip. My eyes fell to her mouth, and it took quite an effort to bring them back to her eyes again.

"You have, uh, some cream cheese on your mouth," she said softly.

I licked my lips, and she made a soft whimpering noise as she watched me hungrily. She hadn't been kidding when she'd said it was hard for her as well to resist me.

"Now?" I asked. Her gaze was transfixed on my lips, and she just shook her head.

"Here, I'll get it," she whispered, stepping towards me.

When her body neared mine, the space between us crackled with electricity. It took everything in me not to pull her to me. Raising her hand to my face, she used her thumb to wipe away the cream cheese. Before she could pull away, I clutched her hand at the wrist and sucked her thumb into my mouth, sucking away the remnants. Her eyes fluttered closed and I studied her face while I softly sucked her thumb.

Finally, her eyes blinked open and she reluctantly pulled her thumb from my mouth but made no moves to step away. We stared at each other, each begging the other with our eyes to make the first move. I wanted her so fucking badly. Her eyes were sad but hungry for me. The light brown color of her skin reddened on her cheeks as I regarded her. My gaze eventually fell back to her mouth, and I quickly had to look away before I broke my promise to keep things at a friendly level.

"You better eat," I said gruffly, and the spell was broken.

She stepped back and snatched up the coffee. Pulling a notepad and pen from a kitchen drawer, she began to make a grocery list. After that, we managed to resist our desires. We spent the next two months doing just that.

Chapter FOURTEEN

Olive

A couple of months later...

"OLIVE, HON, TILT your head a little more to the right," Sophie the photographer ordered.

Leaning over, I remained still as she shot a few more pictures.

"Okay, sweetie. I think I've got enough. You did great. Beautiful as always," she gushed before walking out of the studio.

My head was pounding and I felt slightly ill because of it. Sliding down to the floor next to my bag, I picked up my bottle of water and sipped it. I'd forgotten to grab breakfast on the way, which had clearly been a mistake.

Pulling my phone from my bag, I dialed Bray. We'd fallen easily into the role of best friends in the last two months. Both of us had made quite an effort to not pounce on one another. Now that we'd spent lots of time together without sex, he'd really become my best friend.

"Hey, love," he said into the phone when he answered. I grinned at his nickname for me.

"Hey! I just finished a shoot and realized I skipped breakfast. Want to grab lunch?" I asked. We typically met several times a week for lunch. Slowly but surely, he was helping me get over my fear of being in public. At first it had been awkward and weird, but eventually I'd gotten used to it. I'd yet to run into Drake, which I had hoped meant that the city was big enough to where I would never have to see him again.

"Of course. Need me to pick you up or do you want to meet somewhere?" he asked.

Scooping up my bag, I headed for the exit. "I'll meet you at the office. I should be there in fifteen minutes," I told him and hung up. It was good that I was meeting him at the office because I needed to talk about Pepper's bridal shower with Andi.

I was still grinning when I rounded the corner from the building and ran right smack into a hard chest. The familiar smell enveloped me and I jerked away from it. Everything spun as my senses were flooded with his scent.

"Ollie?" the voice asked. My knees went weak and the world tilted. How in the world had I managed to run into him?

"Leave me alone," I hissed as I backed away from him. His hand reached out, grabbing my wrist, and I nearly threw up.

"Ollie, I've missed you so much," he said sadly.

Pulling from my newfound confidence, I yanked my hand from his grasp, surprising both of us. "Don't ever touch me again, Drake," I spat at him, turning on my heels and heading straight for a waiting cab.

"I'll see you soon, Ollie," he called after me, successfully sending a fit of chills through my body.

After throwing myself into the cab, I refused to look at him as it pulled away from the curb.

"Let's do it at her parents' house," Andi suggested. I was standing at her desk, waiting for Bray to get off the phone. We were still trying to hash out the details for a bridal shower for our newly engaged friend.

"That's a good idea. Her family will know where to go and Sandra would love to have it there," I agreed.

"Olive," Bray said behind me, poking me in the ribs. I yelped but giggled when I turned around and saw his boyish grin.

"Ready, dork?" I asked, picking up my purse. He slung his arm over my shoulder. I still shuddered any time he touched me, but I was getting better at hiding it.

"Yep, crazy girl," he teased.

Andi laughed at our banter. She'd grown used to our friendship. If anything, she was happy I'd found a friend to hang out with since she and Pepper were so busy with their own men. Bray and I had never spoken to her about our brief romantic spell together.

Once we got into the elevator, Bray spoke.

"Okay, what's up? You're going through the motions, but I can tell you're upset about something. Did the photo shoot not go well?" he asked, looking down at me. I sighed heavily, suddenly feeling ill again. He really did know me well and could read my emotions so easily.

"Bray, I ran into Drake," I replied, lip trembling. He spun me around to face him, hands tightly gripping my shoulders.

"What the fuck, Olive? Did he talk to you?" he demanded anxiously.

"Yeah. He seemed pretty happy to see me. He said he'd see me around," I choked out, bile rising in my throat. Suddenly, I felt lightheaded and gripped his waist.

"I won't let him hurt you," he promised.

The elevator spun wildly and everything went black.

"Olive!" Bray shouted, pulling me back into consciousness. I blinked my eyes several times, feeling confused. The room was still spinning. Bray was holding me to him, which was good because my knees felt weak.

"I think I might be sick," I groaned. When the elevator stopped at the garage level, I barely made it out before I emptied the contents of my stomach all over the concrete just outside the elevator.

"Olive, I'm taking you home. What's wrong? Did Drake make you that upset?" he asked, rubbing my back.

"I think it's a combination of things. This morning I skipped breakfast. Once I saw Drake, I instantly started to feel worse. I'll probably be okay once I eat," I said shakily. He nodded and helped me into his car.

We went straight to my apartment, where he settled me on the couch. Bray got busy in the kitchen and emerged with some soup, crackers, and a glass of clear soda.

"You can't skip meals, Olive. Surely you've learned from Andi and the way she gets when she doesn't eat," he chided, setting the food down in front of me.

"I know. I was just in a hurry. It was probably more the Drake thing than the lack of food," I confessed. His face darkened at the mention of Drake again.

I slowly ate my soup and started feeling better immediately. Bray watched me the entire time.

"Bray, you should eat something too. You still have to go back to work," I told him.

He frowned but made no moves to get up. "I'm not going back to work today. I can afford to take half a day to look after you," he stated simply and went to the kitchen to make a sandwich.

Rolling my eyes, I went and brushed my teeth to get the acidic taste out of my mouth. He was polishing off his sandwich when I made it back to the room. Patting the cushion beside him, he motioned for me to sit.

"How do you feel now?" he asked once I plopped down. I

curled up next to him and let him put his arm around me.

"Much better. You're too good to me," I replied, leaning into him.

Stroking my arm, he kissed the top of my head. Feeling in-credibly tired, I fell asleep.

Chapter FIFTEEN

Bray

SHE FELL ASLEEP on me, and I seethed with anger. If that asshole was stalking her, I would fucking kill him. It worried the hell out of me that she'd run into him. Scooping her up, I toted her to her bedroom and put her under the covers.

Walking out to the living room, I called Jordan.

"Hey, man. I'm not coming back to the office. Olive is sick so I want to look after her."

"No problem, Bray. We'll see you tomorrow," he said easily.

"I want to talk to you about something. Do you remember that PI Pepper's dad used?" I questioned.

"Yeah, I have his contact info I can send you. Might I ask why you need it?"

"You can't tell Pepper or anyone. I don't want Olive knowing I told you this or she'll be pissed at me. Her ex nearly killed her several months ago. She ran into him today. I believe, if given the chance, he'll follow through with it. I want to protect her," I explained.

He grunted angrily at my words. "That explains a lot about why she is the way she is. I'll email you the information. This fucking sucks, Bray. I can relate, considering all we went through with Elizabeth and that crazy-ass Cole. I'm sorry, man," he huffed into the phone.

"Me too, Jordan. I will always protect her. If I ever run into that asshole, he better run fast the other way because I'm going to beat the fucking shit out of him," I spat furiously.

"And I'll fucking help," Jordan agreed.

We hung up and I went back in there to Olive. Crawling in beside her, I put my arm around her. We might not be romantically involved, but we spent a lot of time together and we almost always had to be touching in some way. I must have woken her up because she rolled over to face me.

"Who were you talking to?" she asked.

"Jordan. I was telling him I wasn't coming in today. Do you feel any better?" I questioned. Her bottom lip poked out slightly and my gaze fell to it. This was the hardest thing about our relationship. There were times when we wanted to do more than cuddle—it was clear to the both of us.

Normally, she would be the first to pull away, but not today. Instead of answering my question, she leaned slightly closer to me. The smell that was hers invaded my senses and I fought not to inhale her. Uncharacteristic for our relationship, she leaned in the rest of the way and softly pecked my lips, leaving them pressed to mine.

We stayed there for a second, lips touching, gazing at one another. Her hand snaked up to my cheek and she grazed it with her thumb. She parted her lips just barely and I slipped my tongue into her mouth. Our tongues softly danced together to a unique rhythm. When she sweetly moaned into my mouth, I lost control.

I drew her to me with the arm that was around her as I deepened our kiss. Two months of fighting our feelings for one another were suddenly tossed aside as we gave in to our suppressed desires. Her hand made its way to the buttons on my shirt and she began undoing them one by one. I pulled away from our kiss for a moment to look into her blazing eyes.

"Olive, I want you so fucking bad. I never stopped wanting you," I confessed.

She smiled broadly at me. "Me too, Bray. Make love to me," she purred as her she batted her dark lashes at me. I leaned her over onto her back and unfastened her jeans. The girl wore shorts a lot at home, but when she wore her tight little jeans, it was the hottest fucking thing on the planet.

Sliding her jeans off, I admired her smooth chocolate-colored thighs. Having forgotten what she tasted like, I leaned over and dragged my tongue up the inside of her thigh, enjoying the sweetness.

"Oh my God, Bray, I missed you so much," she moaned. Even though we'd seen each other every day for the last couple of months, I knew she meant that she missed me in this way. Grabbing her panties, I jerked them down her legs and off of her.

She sat up and pulled off her top, no longer embarrassed for me to see her marred skin. Her bra quickly followed. I finished unbuttoning my shirt and tossed it and my undershirt away from me. When I sat up on my knees to undo the button on my slacks, she knelt in front of them and unfastened them for me. Pushing my pants and boxers down my thighs, she freed my cock and stroked it with both hands.

Her perfect palms rubbed me almost into coming immediately.

"Baby, I missed this so badly that if you keep touching me like that, I'm going to come all over your belly in another few seconds," I groaned. She smiled saucily at me. Saucy was a good look on Olive.

"Get rid of the pants and lie on your back," she commanded. Bossy Olive was fucking hot too.

Complying, I did as I was told and laid back on the bed.

She positioned herself between my legs and bent over me.

Grasping my dick in both hands, she tentatively licked the tip.

"Fuck," I moaned, grabbing her hair. Olive took that as reassurance and sucked my entire cock into her mouth. She felt so fucking good as she teased, licked, and sucked me like I tasted amazing.

"Babe, I'm about to come," I warned, expecting her to take her mouth off of me. But she was encouraged and she sucked me hard until my release burst from me. Olive swallowed until my dick stopped throbbing in her mouth. Once I was finished, she pulled away with a grin.

"I've waited so long to do that," she admitted. She looked absolutely beautiful and glowing after her present to me. Clearly she was proud of her abilities. I was fucking impressed as hell.

"Your turn," I growled, pulling her to me. She squealed when I rolled her over to her back. Kneeling down between her, I licked up her slit and she bucked her ass off the bed from the contact to her clit.

"Bray," she moaned.

I licked her again slowly. When she grabbed handfuls of my hair and pulled me to her shaven pussy, I picked up the pace. Sliding my longest finger inside her, I located her g-spot and stroked it while I tongued her sensitive flesh.

"Ohmygod," she rushed out, exhaling sharply as her body convulsed with an orgasm. I could feel the walls of her sex clench around my finger with each pulse of her aftershocks. When she finally settled down, I pulled my finger from her and looked over her beautiful body.

The angry scars across her belly made me hate Drake more and more each time I saw them. She must have been terrified for her life and in so much pain. I would like to carve his fucking face.

She was watching my face as it went from desire to fury in seconds. I dragged my eyes away from the words scarred across her torso and revered her perky tits. Leaning over to one of them, I licked her nipple and sucked it into my mouth.

"Ouch. A little rough," she whimpered, pushing my head away. I looked at her quizzically but dipped back down and kissed it gently the next time. When my lips made their way to her neck, she whined and wrapped her legs around my hips in an attempt to get me inside her.

"Hold on a sec," I panted as I quickly hopped off of her and found a condom in my wallet. She grinned at me as I sheathed my dick and climbed back between her legs.

With my hand, I guided my dick into her, slowly letting it get covered in her wetness before I began thrusting in and out of her. She felt so fucking good, and the walls of her pussy gripped my dick as if it didn't want to let it go. Her panting picked up speed as I quickly plunged in and out.

When she scratched my back as her orgasm shuddered through her, I came quickly from the combination of the roughness and the clenching of her pussy. Spent, I collapsed over her, resting on my elbows.

"Olive," I said, kissing her lips briefly.

"Mmmm?" she asked, completely sated.

"Why have we been fighting this connection? I only want to be with you. You're all I've thought about since the day we met. Please tell me we can be together," I practically begged.

"Bray, you're all I think about as well. I think you are a great friend, but I want more than that with you. With you, I want the whole package. My only concern is breaking it to Andi. I think she's used to the idea of us being together so much already. Maybe we should—" She was interrupted by the bedroom door flinging open.

"Olive, Jordan said you were sick—what the fuck?!" Pepper exclaimed once she realized Olive and I were obviously in the middle of a sexual moment. Instead of backing out of the room, she was glaring at us.

Yanking the covers over us, I met her glare with one of my own. "Pepper, do you fucking mind? We'll be in the living room in a minute. Give us a second to put some fucking clothes on first," I spat at her.

She looked absolutely livid. After she backed out of the room, shaking her head, and slammed the door behind her, I turned to look at Olive.

"Shit, babe. I'm sorry she walked in on us. Are you okay?" I asked.

She nodded, resolved to finally let the cat out of the bag. "I'm ready to tell everyone and get it over with. Bray, I'm tired of hiding how much I care about you. I want to hold your hand in public without fear of someone finding out. We shouldn't have to hide this," she affirmed.

Leaning over, I kissed her deeply. I was tired of keeping my feelings for her under a lid as well.

"Let's do this," I said reassuringly as I rolled off of her and began to dress.

Chapter SIXTEEN

Olive

WHEN WE WALKED into the living room, Pepper stood from the recliner and glared at us. Not being able to meet her stare, I looked down at my feet.

"You two have some fucking explaining to do," she spoke, barely able to keep the anger from her voice.

"Olive and I met the night of Andi's birthday party. We hit it off immediately. After spending some time together romantically, we decided to keep our relationship to just friends in an effort to not hurt Andi. The two of us have been strictly friends for two months now, but we decided we want to be more than that. Andi will understand. I know it," he explained. I grabbed his hand and squeezed it supportively. Risking a glance at Pepper, I cringed when she pinned me with her furious stare.

"Well whooptie-fucking-do! You think because you guys *decided* that you want to be together that things are perfectly fine now? Olive, you weren't fucking there when Andi almost DIED from her depression!" she shouted.

"*I* was, Pepper, and it was fucking horrible! Andi is stronger now than she was when we broke up. She *will* be okay!" Bray yelled back.

Ignoring him, she turned to me again. "You. She fucking took you in off the street and you turn around and fuck her ex-fiancé the moment she turns her back. The ex-fiancé that cheated on her. The ex-fiancé that nearly made her kill herself. How fucking low could you go? Pack your shit and get out of my apartment. There is no fucking way I'm letting you hurt her, because once again, I'll be the one left to fix her," she spat hatefully. "He'll just cheat on you too. Once a cheater, always a cheater."

My mouth gaped open as tears stung my eyes. She glanced over at me, and even though she was pissed, I could tell she regretted what she'd said. When she crossed her arms angrily, she slightly winced. She'd recently had surgery on her wrist and was sporting a pink bandage. I was mesmerized by the thing until Bray's voice snapped me back to the present.

"Pepper, you were always such a bitch. Olive's better without someone like you in her life," Bray growled over at her, dragging me back to my room.

I heard the apartment door slam shut. Bursting into tears, I let Bray hold me as I cried.

"Bray, this is exactly what I was afraid of. If Pepper is this pissed, maybe we didn't think things through," I said sadly, sniffling.

"Hell no. Don't let her make you feel bad. I'm going to fucking call Andi right now and tell her. This is fucking stupid to hide this from her. Pepper is blowing it way out of proportion," he declared loudly, still riled up over our fight with Pepper.

"No! Please, Bray. Let me tell her in person. I hope Pepper doesn't tell her. God, I feel like I'm going to throw up," I shakily told him, bolting to the bathroom. He hurried after me, holding my hair back as I emptied my lunch into the toilet.

"Shit, Olive. What the fuck is wrong with you? I'm taking you to the doctor. You clearly have a stomach bug or something. If stress is doing this to you, I will be so fucking pissed. Between us, Drake, and Pepper, you are getting yourself too overworked," he said anxiously.

I didn't say anything back to him. Hugging the toilet, I tried not to worry about everything.

"Olive?" he asked quietly.

Turning my head, I looked into his beautiful blue eyes. They were regarding me with an unreadable emotion.

"Olive, is there any way you could be pregnant? We were both pretty shitfaced that first time and I don't remember using protection," he explained softly.

My mind reeled at his proclamation. Instantly I thought about the baby I'd lost when I left Drake. It would explain the sickness and tender breasts. If Pepper was pissed about us being together, she was going to be livid if I was carrying his baby. *Bray's baby.* For some reason, my heart soared at the possibility. A tear trickled out and rolled down my cheek.

"There's a good possibility since I'm not on any type of birth control. They make me gain a lot of weight, and with modeling, I couldn't handle the weight fluctuations so I don't use them," I admitted.

Several looks crossed his face, and I chewed my lip nervously. Finally, he broke into a grin.

"That would be better than an illness or stress," he told me, eyes twinkling. I couldn't help but smile broadly back at him.

He suddenly jumped up and went into the other room. When he came back into the bathroom, he had on his coat and shoes.

"Where are you going?" I questioned.

"I'm running to the drugstore to buy a pregnancy test," he beamed at me.

My heart fluttered as I realized how happy this had made him.

Thirty minutes later, we sat on the bathroom counter waiting for the test to produce its results. Bray had bought the test that was digital and said plainly whether or not you were pregnant. No confusing blue lines to contend with.

"What's it say?" he asked excitedly.

When I picked it up from the counter, my jaw dropped as I read the results.

"It says you're going to be a daddy," I gasped in disbelief. I turned to look at him, and he was grinning like a fool.

Putting both hands on my cheeks, he brought his face to mine and kissed me tenderly. "Olive, I'm so fucking happy right now. You're moving in with me—end of story. I'm going to take care of you and my baby," he said sweetly. His hand made its way to my belly and he rubbed it gently. It was incredibly intimate and sweet.

"Me too, Bray. I'm so happy too. I do want to be with you. As happy as I am about the baby though, I'm really upset about Pepper. What am I going to do about it?" I asked sadly.

"We're going to sit down and talk to Andi about it. Let's invite her and Jackson over for dinner tonight. She might be upset, but there's nothing we can do about it. We want to be with each other, and if they care about us, they'll be understanding. We're having a baby together. If they want to be a part of its life, then they'll have to be okay with it."

Andi, Jackson, and I were all sitting at the kitchen table of my soon-to-no-longer-be-my-apartment when Bray walked in with the takeout. He distributed it all and sat down with us.

"So I was thinking we could do this theme for her bridal shower," Andi said, holding up a picture on her phone for me to see. I cringed because I wasn't sure how to tell her that Pepper and I had had a major blowup about her.

"Yes, I like that. We could make those," I told her, pointing to the party favors. She nodded, grinning.

After we finished eating, Bray cleared his throat, grabbing their attention, and my tummy did a flip-flop in anticipation.

"Listen, guys. We wanted you to come to dinner because we needed to discuss something with you, Andi," he said quietly.

Andi and Jackson exchanged a look. He'd already visibly tensed up. She looked incredibly nervous.

"Andi, you know we would never intentionally hurt you. Fuck, I'm just going to come out and say it. Olive and I are together," he huffed out.

Andi was silent for a moment as she looked back and forth between us. I pleaded with my eyes for her to understand.

Calmly, much different than Pepper's reaction, she reached over and took my hand into hers. "Olive, I'm happy for you guys," she said honestly. I exhaled loudly and grinned. "You two have been inseparable for two months. I kind of had a clue. It makes me happy for you guys to have each other."

I turned to Bray, who was cheesing with an 'I told you so' look on his face.

"I have Jackson now and even though he can be a prick, he's my prick. Right, Jackie?" she asked, sending him a wink. He grumbled his affirmation, clearly unhappy with our announcement.

"Andi, I love you. We have something else to tell you though," I said, now growing excited. She smiled happily. "Bray and I are going to have a baby."

She squealed and jumped from her chair, nearly tackling me with a hug. Jackson just sat quietly with his arms crossed, frowning. Obviously he didn't share the same feelings as her. Bray was watching him from across the table, his jaw clicking.

"Olive, this is so freaking exciting! When are you going to tell Pepper? She'll be so happy!" she babbled. I sighed as I prepared myself to tell her the next part.

"She sort of walked in on us today and learned it on her own. To say she's pissed is an understatement. She kicked me out of the apartment. Looks like I'll be moving in with Bray. Even though she doesn't live here, her dad still pays the rent."

"What? She kicked you out? Knowing you were pregnant? What's wrong with that girl?" she asked angrily.

Bray shook his head, still pissed with Pepper.

"She's worried about you just like Bray and I were. I think catching us in the act was a surprise, and she didn't take it well. Plus, I didn't know I was pregnant yet when she came over. I'm just so glad you don't hate me," I confessed.

She grinned at me. "Of course I don't hate you. I know Bray is a different person than he was back then. Plus, I love Jackson, so I only want for you and Bray to be happy. Olive, you've been so lonely and afraid since the moment I met you. These last two months, you've been going out more often and seem so happy. Bray is the cause of it, so I could never be upset about it. I'm going to be an aunt!" she squealed.

We hugged again, and I felt like a huge weight had been lifted. Bray and Jackson were still glaring daggers at each other. Those two had issues to work out.

Our conversation quickly turned from weddings to babies. The only thing that was missing was Pepper, and I felt sick about it.

Chapter SEVENTEEN

Bray

"MOM, I WOULD like you to come over for dinner tonight," I told my mother on the phone the next day. Ever since our conversation about Olive a couple of months ago, she'd assumed I had dropped her and moved on. I hadn't talked about her to my mother. She was going to be in for a surprise.

"Well, son, why don't we just meet at our favorite restaurant? No sense in you cooking anything for just the two of us," she told me.

I looked at the design on my computer and made a quick change on something before answering her. "Mom, I'm seeing someone. I thought you could get to know her in a more intimate setting. We can still order food from there. I'll pick it up on the way home," I suggested.

She went quiet for a moment. Quiet was never a good sign when it came to my mother.

"Hmmm," she said as she analyzed what I was saying. Mom was a smart cookie. I could practically hear the wheels turning in her head. "Okay, sweetie. I'll meet you at your place around six then." We hung up and I tapped my pen nervously on the desk.

Olive didn't know that Mom already didn't like her based on

our prior conversation. Mom didn't know that the person I was seeing was Olive. This probably wasn't going to end well, but I didn't see any other way to get through it. It was pissing me off that all of these people were so damned disapproving of our relationship. Olive was worth fighting for, so they could all go to hell.

"Bray, here's a new client file I started for you. The meeting notes are included as well as the pictures of the lot." Andi tossed a folder on my desk. "What's got you making that face?" she asked, laughing.

"Dinner with Mom and Olive tonight. This will be the first time for them to meet," I told her, rubbing my stubbly cheeks with my hands.

"Well I don't see why that would have you stressed looking. Olive is a sweetheart. Everyone loves her. Connie will eat her up," she told me knowingly. "Plus, once she gets wind of a grandbaby, she'll go nuts."

"Andi, there may be a slight problem. See, when Olive and I got together a couple of months ago, I told Mom. She flipped her shit because I finally told her what happened with me and you. Of course she thought Olive was a terrible person and told me to end it with her. We pretty much did end things romantically until yesterday. Mom doesn't know that the woman I'm seeing is Olive," I explained.

She frowned and crossed her arms. "Great, so now Connie is going to freak out once she realizes you're with Olive? Can't you just tell her I'm fine with it all? I don't understand why everyone is so upset about it. Even Jackson is angry with the two of you. I'm going to figure out a way to get the girls together so they can talk it out. Pepper overreacted."

"I don't know, Andi. What's even worse is that Olive will be blindsided. I never told her about what Mom said. It would only hurt her feelings. I just hope Mom has enough respect for me that she won't be rude to her," I sighed.

"I'm sorry, Bray," she said, coming over to my chair. Leaning over, she hugged my neck.

"Wish me luck," I teased, and we both laughed.

"You guys having fun?" Jackson asked irritably from my doorway. Andi jerked away and sauntered over to him. He hugged her but glared at me while he did it. That guy was such a dick.

"I always have fun with your girlfriend," I said, hoping to push his buttons. He muttered something while Andi pushed him out of my office, but not before throwing an annoyed look in my direction. I still wondered what she saw in that guy.

My phone rang and I grinned when Olive's face popped up on the screen.

"Hey," I said, happy to hear her voice.

"Hey, Bray. I was going to let you know I called the doctor. They had a cancellation this morning and could get me in at two. I know it's last minute, but I thought you might want to go. If you're busy, I can go by myself. No big deal," she sputtered out in a rush. I loved the excited edge her voice carried.

"Of course I'll be there. Do you want to meet me there or should I pick you up?" I asked.

"I know you'll need to get back to work, so I'll just grab a cab there. You can run me home after if you want."

"Okay, babe. See you in a bit," I told her, and we hung up.

"And that there is your baby," the doctor told us, pointing to the screen. She was using a wand internally since the baby was still small. Olive had already taken the urine test, which indicated her positive pregnancy, in the office. She was smiling blissfully at the monitor while I was trying to figure out why our blob baby looked like an alien.

"Nothing on that screen looks like a baby," I told her

honestly. They both laughed.

"Well, sir, the baby is still very small. I gave Miss Redding a packet of information. In one of those pamphlets, you can see pictures of what your baby looks like at each stage. That might be helpful for you," the doctor informed me.

I nodded and kept squinting at the screen, trying to make sense of the picture.

"What's that blinking area?" I asked.

"That would be your baby's heartbeat," she said before turning a knob, filling the room with a beating sound.

Olive turned to me with tears in her eyes. "Our baby," she whispered. The sound was beautiful, and I frowned when the doctor turned the speaker back off. I would never get tired of hearing that sound.

"You're a couple months along. The baby is due on September twelfth. We'll see you in a month, Miss Redding," the doctor said. After printing something from the computer, she handed me a picture. My heart swelled when I realized it was our little alien blob. Olive grinned when I showed it to her.

After Olive dressed, we left the office hand in hand. I'd never understood the pregnancy glow until now. Olive didn't just glow, she fucking shone. Her smile had been a continuous one since the moment we'd found out.

Stepping out of the building, we were hit with a blast of icy February air. Pulling her to me, I kissed her forehead.

"How is it possible to love something so tiny already?" she asked dreamily. Her lips glistened, and in that moment, I wanted nothing more than to pull one into my mouth and suck on it.

Fighting the urge to do just that, I answered her. "That's our baby, love. I love little AB too," I agreed, smiling.

"A.B.?" she asked, sounding puzzled. I laughed because she probably wouldn't like my nickname.

"Alien Blob," I chuckled.

She tickled my ribs and pushed me away. "God, you are such a dork," she said, strolling to the car, leaving me to admire the view of her ass.

Chapter EIGHTEEN

Olive

I GLANCED AT the mirror for the hundredth time this evening. Bray's mother would be here soon and I wanted to look my best. Since my relationship with Momma had been severed, I at least wanted our child to be close to one grandparent. My nerves were on overdrive, making my sensitive stomach churn uneasily.

"Olive, relax," Bray instructed. "She'll love you." He walked over to me and placed his hands on my hips. I rested my head on his chiseled chest. He was rubbing circles on my hipbones with his thumbs, and suddenly I wanted him very badly.

I kissed his collarbone, which was exposed just above the top of his sweater. His thumbs made their way up my body and stroked my skin under my shirt just above the waistline of my jeans. I was starting to throb for him. Dragging my tongue up his neck, I found a fleshy part of him and sucked it into my mouth.

He groaned and pulled me close to him. I could feel his hardened cock pressing against me. My hands slithered around the back of his neck and gripped his hair. He dipped his head down and met my lips with his before we hungrily kissed each other.

His hands slid around to my ass and gripped me hard. I gasped.

"Olive, I'm going to fuck you hard. I want to be inside you so badly," he growled, biting at my lip with his teeth. He jerked away and grabbed my hand, drawing me hastily to the bedroom. Once inside with the bedroom door shut behind us, he didn't waste time and unfastened my jeans, pushing them down my thighs. While he fumbled with his pants, I yanked mine the rest of the way off.

When he easily picked me up, I wrapped my legs around his hips and he rammed his cock into me.

"Bray!" I screamed in pleasure. His cock filled up every inch of me and my pussy clenched every time he pounded into me. Bouncing on his length, I could feel my orgasm reaching towards me. When he pulled one hand from gripping my ass to thumb my clit, I completely lost it and my body convulsed with shudders from my orgasm.

"Oh, baby," he groaned as he followed quickly after. I waited until he'd finished pumping into me before I slid down off of him. He hurried into the bathroom to grab a washcloth to clean us up with.

"Come on. Let's hurry before your mom gets here," I said, grabbing my jeans and pulling them on. He quickly dressed knowing we were running out of time. Walking hand in hand, we exited his bedroom only to see his mother sitting primly on the sofa.

"Mom!" he exclaimed when he saw her sitting there.

Her face morphed from shock to anger when she saw me. My cheeks burned from embarrassment, knowing she had heard us loud and clear. Standing from the sofa, she came over to Bray and gave him a hug. Recovering, he cleared his throat.

"Mom, I'd like for you to meet my girlfriend, Olive. Olive, this is my mother, Connie," he spoke nervously.

She flinched at my name and jerked her gaze back to mine. "Nice to meet you," she said coldly.

I raised my hand to shake hers but dropped it once I realized she had no intention of shaking it. Bray was glaring at her because of her blatant rudeness. Not giving him a moment to say anything, she turned on her heel and strode into the kitchen.

"I'm sorry, Olive," he mouthed to me, and I swallowed back the disappointment of the distaste his mother already had towards me. I had experience with disapproving mothers though, so I would smile through it. We followed her into the kitchen.

"How's Andi?" she asked Bray, pretending I wasn't in the room. Shaking his head, he pulled a few plates down from the cabinet and slammed them down, rattling them. Both Connie and I jumped at his sudden anger.

"Dammit, Mom! Get over this. Andi is fine. Olive is here with us and you've barely said two words to her. She is my girl-friend, whom I deeply care about. If you can't get over your atti-tude, then please just go home," he growled. My heart swelled at his protectiveness over me.

Connie's mouth gaped open and I stared at my feet. The awk-wardness of the situation was overwhelming. Risking a glance at her, I saw that she was watching me with guilt written all over her face.

"I'm sorry, Olive. This just took me by surprise is all. It's very nice to meet you, honey."

"Nice to meet you too, ma'am. Bray's a great guy."

"Crumbs! Don't call me ma'am. Please just call me Connie," she laughed. Her features lit up, reminding me of Bray. Maybe this wouldn't be so bad after all.

"Connie, can I get you something to drink?" I asked, hoping to keep the mood light.

"I'll take a glass of Merlot, honey," she smiled.

Skirting around her, I pulled two glasses from the under cab-inet rack and poured the wine that was sitting on the counter. I grabbed a bottle of water from the refrigerator for myself.

Once we sat down with our plates of food, Connie started

telling a funny story about Bray's dad, Jim. Apparently he was a crotchety man who enjoyed staying in the confines of their home. I could relate.

"So, Olive, what nationality are you? I never expected Bray to date a black girl," she said rather bluntly, making me choke on my water.

Bray's eyes grew huge as he gasped in exasperation. "Mom! Does your candor know no bounds?"

"What, Bray? It's a legitimate question. She's got the lightest brown skin I've seen on a black girl. Her eyes are so pale. Those cheeks of hers turn rosy red when she's embarrassed, which appears to be often. I just want to know how she came to look like this. Olive, you're a beautiful girl, by the way," she winked at me. Bray rolled his eyes at her, but I could see the interest in his eyes to know a little bit more about me.

"My mother is African-American and my father is Caucasian. He left her once she was pregnant with me, but that's how I came to have this fair skin and light-colored eyes."

"I see. Honey, did you not want any wine?" she asked, just now realizing I was drinking water.

My cheeks burned, and I instantly felt guilty because she'd just mentioned my obvious blushing. Bray and I exchanged nervous looks.

"Mom, I need to tell you something." He pulled my hand into his lap under the table and squeezed it. She frowned at the serious look on his face. "Olive is pregnant. We're going to have a baby in September," he rushed out.

Her eyes nearly bugged out of her head and her jaw dropped open. "But you aren't even married. You just started dating!" she exclaimed. Snatching up her glass, she downed the entire thing.

"Connie, we conceived a couple of months ago. We're both happy about this," I supplied, hoping to erase the sick look on her face.

"Of course *you* are happy about this. Since you won't be able to model anymore, you'll latch on to my successful Brayden. Life will be perfect for Olive. *Of course you're happy,*" she snapped. Tears sprung to my eyes. This woman was insufferable.

"Mom!" Bray roared, startling Connie and me.

She just glared back at him. "Bray, you don't have to be with her just because she's pregnant. I know how your mind works. You think you need to save her. Just because you got her pregnant doesn't mean you have to force a relationship. You can still pay child support and be a part of the baby's life. But you don't have to stay with her," she spat.

Hastily standing up from my chair, I rushed into the living room. Their words had become heated and were growing louder. I walked back into the room, clutching my purse.

Bray's eyes widened in surprise. "Babe, please don't leave," he pled, standing. Connie's mouth quirked up in a smile as she thought she'd succeeded in running me off.

"I'm not leaving, Bray. Here," I told Connie as I thrust the sonogram in her face. "This is your grandbaby. A sweet little baby that is half of your son. We love this precious being. If you want to be a part of this baby's life, I suggest you lose the attitude. I won't have my child around this negativity[MR1]," I told her fiercely.

My hands were quivering but I mentally high-fived myself for bravely standing up to her. She grew quiet as she stared at the picture. When she finally looked back up at me, her eyes were glistening with tears. Bray walked over to her and put his hand on her shoulder.

"Mom, meet A.B." He grinned and winked at me. I smiled back at him. The way he boasted about our little baby filled my heart with happiness.

"A.B.?" she questioned, looking up at him.

Chuckling, he told her, "Alien Blob."

"Brayden! Don't call my grandbaby an alien!" she scolded, but the grin was plastered all over her face. "Olive, I'm sorry—again. This is just a lot to take in. Give me some time to acclimate myself to all of this, but I promise I'll come around," she told me in apology.

I just smiled shyly at her and nodded.

"Okay, kids. It's getting late. I need to get home to feed Jim. But first"—she pulled her iPhone from her pocket—"I need to make A.B. my screensaver," she grinned as she snapped a picture of the sonogram. "Granny needs to show Poppy his grandchild."

She looked pleased at appointing herself as Granny. The earlier tense moment lifted as she gathered her purse. I was surprised when she pulled me in for a hug.

"Don't hurt my boy," she whispered into my ear before pulling away, and I shivered at her warning.

Chapter NINETEEN

Bray

ONCE MOM FINALLY left, I turned to Olive, feeling awful about the entire dinner.

"Babe, I'm so sorry about all of that. My mother is great once you make it through her tough exterior. Ask Andi—she knows firsthand. I'm sorry she said those things to you. I really care about you and I'm excited to be having this baby with you. Tomorrow we can move some of your things over here."

She looked at me with sadness in her eyes, making me feel sick about the way my mother had treated her. Her own mother wouldn't have anything to do with her and now mine was giving her a hard time. Grabbing her hand, I led her over to the sofa, where we sat down beside each other.

"Bray, I'm not using you. I can find an apartment. There's no sense in you feeling obligated to take me in. I probably won't show for a little while longer and then I can get a job waiting tables or something. And honestly, I send my mom most of my modeling money anyway and she never cashes those checks. I bet I have quite a nest egg saved up."

"Fuck that!" I growled, causing her to flinch. Reaching over, I pulled her light frame into my lap. Instinctively, she settled a leg on either side of my hips. "Olive, there is no way I'm letting my pregnant girlfriend wait fucking tables. I want to wake up every morning as I watch your belly swell with my child inside. You aren't an obligation to me."

She nodded but still seemed unconvinced. Her eyes misted over, but she quickly blinked them away. Between Pepper and now my mother, Olive was feeling like the bad guy. It was one thing for them to be pissed at me, but I saw red when they treated Olive the way they had been.

Olive's phone rang from her back pocket. When she went to answer it, I took the moment to distract her from her sadness by teasing her nipple with my teeth through her shirt. Grabbing a handful of her ass with each hand, I pulled her against my already throbbing, hard cock. She nearly whimpered as she answered her phone.

"Hello?" she asked, distracted as I continued to touch her. When her body became rigid, I looked up at her and stopped my caresses. She was frowning and seemed worried as hell. "Opal, slow down. Where are you? I can come get you but you need to tell me where you're at."

I could hear a hysterical female voice on the other end. Olive was listening intently. She finally spoke again.

"I know all about abusive boyfriends. Tell me where you are and I'll come get you."

Suddenly Olive dropped the phone into my lap. She looked incredibly ill as she practically ran into the kitchen, barely making it to the sink before she vomited. I picked up the phone.

"Opal? This is Bray, Olive's boyfriend. What's going on?"

I'd never spoken to her but I felt like I knew her since Olive talked about her so often. Olive adored her baby sister. And unfortunately, because of their mother, the two hadn't been able to see each other. Olive had hoped that since Opal had turned eighteen recently, things would change.

"I was just telling Olive my address. Where did she go?" she asked tearfully. The girl sounded panicked. Extremely panicked. The hair on my neck prickled.

"Tell me the address, Opal. We're coming to get you." I hopped up and hurried into my third bedroom, which I use for an office. Locating a pad of paper and a pen, I asked her to give it to me. I scrawled out the address and asked her to repeat it to make sure I'd written it down correctly.

"Hurry! He'll wake up soon," she whispered.

"I can be there in fifteen minutes. Hang tight."

I hung up and found Olive still bent over the sink in the kitchen.

"Babe, are you okay?" I asked. She shook her head back and forth as she looked ready to heave some more. While rubbing her back, I quickly called Andi. "Andi, let me talk to Jackson," I demanded when she answered the phone.

Understanding that my tone was a serious one, she didn't argue, passing it on to a voice that was gruff when it answered.

"Jackson, I'm going to text you an address. Meet me there. Get over there as soon as you can. Send Andi over here to my place to stay with Olive—she's sick and I'd hate to leave her alone. I'll text you my address as well."

I would have called Jordan, but since Pepper was being a bitch to Olive, I would have to deal with Jackson instead. Surprising me, he grunted that he'd be there and hung up. After quickly texting him the addresses, I wrapped my arms around Olive and kissed the back of her head.

"Andi is coming to stay with you. I'm going to get Opal for you. Will you be okay?"

I pulled away from her to grab my keys and wallet. When she turned to look at me, I was chilled by the haunted, wild look in her eyes.

"Bring me my purse," she rasped out, her voice scratchy from vomiting. I went into the living room and brought it back to her. She dug through it and produced a key.

"You're going to need this," she tells me softly.

I grabbed the key from her as things started rapidly falling into place. Nodding, I kissed her forehead once more before bolting out the front door. Things had just gotten more serious, and I needed to get Opal out of there quickly.

Minutes later, I was in my car and hauling ass to the address I'd programmed into my GPS. When I pulled up to the apartment building and found a spot, I was pleased to see Jackson already there, leaning against the building.

"Want to tell me what the fuck is going on?" he grumbled.

"Olive's sister Opal is in trouble. She's here and we need to get her out as soon as possible," I told him as we walked quickly into the building. Once we were at the door of the address Opal gave me, I produced the key from my pocket.

"What are you doing?" Jackson hissed.

Ignoring him, I quietly unlocked the door and walked into the dark apartment. Jackson followed cautiously behind me. My eyes scanned the living room only to find it empty. I took soft steps toward the end of the hallway, where dim light shone through under the closed doorway. Once there, I gingerly turned the knob and peeked inside.

My stomach flip-flopped at the sight. A naked young woman sat shivering on the floor beside the bed. One hand was bound my some sort of rope to the bed post. Her free hand clutched a cell phone. A large, naked black man lay facedown on the bed, snoring. When her eyes met mine, I saw nothing but relief. A long, slender finger covered her lip, indicating for me to be quiet. Nodding my understanding, I opened the door enough to get inside the room.

I turned to Jackson and saw that he was glaring angrily at the situation. Without words, he started snatching up her clothes from the floor while I quickly set to work at freeing her hand. Tears were silently streaming down her cheeks. Finally, I loosened the rope enough that she was able to slip her hand through. She rubbed it for a second before attempting to stand. I grabbed her elbows and stood her up. Her body shook violently so I didn't release my hold. Jackson helped dress her while I made sure she didn't collapse.

It was in that moment that I realized she had been roughed up. Dried blood was caked on one corner of her busted bottom lip. More was smeared around her nose. Her hair was wild and all over the place. The rat bastard on the bed had done this to her.

I clenched my teeth and was about to jump on the bed to break the fucker's neck when Jackson's eyes met mine. He shook his head, silently telling me not to do what I was thinking. With a reluctant nod, I got over that notion and we started helping Opal to the door. When a groan came from the bed, Opal yelped out in fear.

"What the fuck?" the voice growled.

In an instant, Jackson scooped Opal into his arms and bolted out the door. I was heading that way when a pair of large hands spun me around.

I was nose to nose with a very large dark-skinned man whose eyes shone wildly with rage. The alcohol on his breath was strong, and he wobbled slightly. He was stark naked, and my eyes couldn't help but hone in on the tattoo scrawled across where his heart was. One simple word: *Olive.*

My vision blurred with hate as my thoughts were confirmed. Rearing back, I punched him forcefully in the jaw, which sent him stumbling back several steps. He tripped over a pair of his shoes and landed hard on his ass. Stalking over to him, I kicked him brutally in the ribs. Kicking him over and over again, I thought of each scar across Olive's belly and it served to fuel my rage.

Falling to my knees, I grabbed his throat and began punching his face repeatedly. I wasn't sure how long I'd been hitting him when a pair of strong arms pulled me away from him.

"That's enough. She's in the car waiting. Let's go," Jackson commanded. He had a firm grip on my upper arm.

Instead of fighting, I let him push me out of the apartment. It wasn't until we'd reached the cool evening air that my head cleared. And suddenly I was ready to finish the job.

"Let me go," I spat at Jackson as I tried to go back upstairs. My body thrummed with the need to kill the man who preyed on innocent women.

"Not a chance. Now get your ass in your car and drive home. We'll follow you."

Conceding, I jerked my arm away and stalked over to my car. Now that I knew where the fucker lived, I had a feeling we'd be seeing each other again. And soon.

Chapter TWENTY

Olive

"THEY'RE ON THEIR way back now, Olive. Jackson just texted me. They have Opal, sweetie. Everything is going to be okay," Andi confirmed.

The message was music to my ears. I was going to have my sister back. There were so many unanswered questions. The main one was driving me crazy. How in the world had Opal ended up with Drake?

She handed me another cracker. Once she had shown up earlier with crackers and ginger ale, I had started to feel lots better. Now, we were huddled together on the sofa while I nibbled crackers.

"Andi, he was a monster," I told her softly.

Her eyes flew to mine. Nobody but Bray knew the story of exactly what kind of monster Drake really was. She squeezed my hand, urging me to go on. Suddenly, I wanted to tell her everything.

"He abused me," I began. Feeling slightly ill, I sipped on the soda before continuing. "At first, it was simple stuff. I'd smile at someone in public and he would get jealous. He would grip my wrist tightly, leaving bruises. In the beginning, I just thought it meant he really cared about me. That he didn't want to share me. It was flattering in some warped way."

I fiddled with the hem of my shirt with my free hand. While with Drake, I'd really lost the sense of what was right and wrong.

"It only got worse—especially when he'd been drinking. He moved on to shaking me or shoving me. Then slapping me. Eventually he would punch and kick me. He controlled everything about me—what I ate, what jobs I took, who I could talk to. I felt trapped but didn't know what to do about it. I was so scared.

"One day, he took it way too far. He hurt me so badly that I ended up in the hospital. That next day, I met you. You were my guardian angel, Andi," I told her.

Tears filled her eyes as she sniffled and pulled me in for a hug. We cried together for a few minutes before we finally broke apart.

"I'm still you're guardian angel. Don't you forget it," she teased.

I smiled at her, but then it fell away sadly. "Andi, that's why I'm so worried about Opal. She somehow ended up with Drake, and I know what he can do. He did this to me," I said and lifted my shirt.

Her eyes flew to my belly. A hand covered her mouth as she gasped.

"What the fuck! Olive, why isn't that fucker in jail?" she exclaimed. I didn't flinch when her fingers delicately traced the outlines of the scars. It was time I'd come to terms with my past. No more hiding from it.

"Honestly, Andi, I thought he would come after me. A successful guy like him with no prior record will just get released on bail. I was worried that he would immediately seek revenge if I turned him in. And up until I met Bray, I had been terrified of running into him. New York seems like a big place until you have a crazy ex that would stop at nothing to reclaim you. Suddenly every shadow and tall, dark-skinned man had me running for the hills. I took up self-defense and now own a gun that I know how to shoot."

"Yeah, I think you proved that with the whole Cole situation," she agreed.

"It wasn't until I met Bray that I felt like I could move on with my life. He was protective and gentle—two things I desperately needed in a man. Problem was, he was your ex. Hooking up with him while we were drunk was such a mistake. We didn't consider your feelings. But once we made that connection, we couldn't turn it off. That's why, even though we chose to be just friends, we couldn't stay away from one another."

Andi smiled and squeezed my hand again. "Babe, I'll be honest. It was weird when I found out, but I wasn't unhappy. Don't tell Jackson, but I'll always love Bray. He was my first love. And even though he made the mistake he did, Bray is still a good person. The fact that he acknowledges his mistake and seems keen on never doing anything of the sort again is huge. Deep in my heart, I always knew he wouldn't do it again. But we were finished and I haven't looked back. We weren't right for each other.

"When we were together, we were mostly like good friends. Always going to ballgames and hanging with our friends at school. Even though we were romantically involved, it wasn't like it is with Jackson. With Jackson, I feel tethered to him. I need him and he needs me. It's on a deeper level than I ever shared with Bray.

"But you and Bray, I most certainly know that your feelings are real. You may have been just 'friends' for the past two months, but I knew it was only a matter of time before you both became an item. There is hardly a moment that you two aren't touching. For two months now, I've observed the way you always seem to look for each other in a room. Like you need the confirmation that your other half is nearby.

"Each time you're together, both of your faces light up with sheer happiness. Bray lost his light a long time ago. I never realized it until I saw it again by the way he looks at you. And you— you have never smiled so much or been so carefree. You guys are good for each other. And our third musketeer will come around eventually. She'll have to."

Tears filled my eyes at the thought of Pepper still being so angry with me.

"Andi, what if I'm not a good mom? My own mother is a horrible example. I'm honestly terrified of letting Bray and the baby down," I sigh sadly.

"Honey, you can stop that thinking right now. Believe me. I know horrible moms. My mother, father, and sister always treated me like the outcast that didn't belong. Some people just don't have a loving bone in their bodies—like my family. But you and I, we're made of the good stuff. We have so much love to give those around us and it's never-ending. You're going to be a great mom, and I assure you I'll be right here to make sure that happens," she winks.

"Andi, I love you."

"I love you too, girl."

A jingle of keys at the door had us both jumping to our feet. Bray flung open the door and held it open as Jackson carried in my beat-up little sister.

"Opal!" I shrieked, running over to them. She turned her head to me and my heart sank. Her face reminded me of my own not too many months ago. Her small hand reached over and touched my cheek. The tears in my eyes blurred my vision, and I quickly blinked them back so I could see her again.

"I've missed you so much," I whispered. She nodded her head, her lip quivering too much to verbally answer me back.

"Jackson, bring her to the guest room," Bray ordered.

Jackson followed him into the room and gingerly laid Opal down on the bed. I crawled in beside her and snaked my arm across her abdomen. She winced, which meant Drake had hurt her there too. When I went to pull my hand away, she held it in place.

"Don't leave me. I'm okay. Just a little sore," she croaked out.

"Opal, I will never leave you."

Andi, Jackson, and Bray all stood around the bed looking down at us. Andi looked worried, but the two men shared the same furious expression.

"What the fuck just happened?" Jackson finally asked, breaking the silence. Opal flinched at his tone, and I suddenly felt protective of her because she was in the same state I'd been in just a few months ago.

"Don't talk to her like that," I snapped at him. Andi elbowed him in the ribs, and his features softened as he realized he was being harsh.

"Shit, sorry. My mind is still reeling from the fact that Bray and I just rescued a damsel in distress from a fucking naked giant," Jackson said as he ran his hands through his hair, obviously confused at the situation.

"Somehow or another, Opal seems to have gotten herself involved with the man who would have killed me had I not made my escape that night. How did you get involved with Drake?" I asked Opal.

"After you left, I missed you so much. Momma didn't understand—thought you were evil. Secretly, I would scour every fashion magazine for you. When I would find one with you in it, I would buy the magazine and cut out the picture. A couple of months ago, an extremely good-looking photographer showed up on the doorstep after school. Momma was at work so I let him in. He told me he was a model scout and had seen some of my pictures on Facebook. In that moment, my heart soared at the possibility of following in your footsteps.

"He told me he would provide room and board if I would come to New York City. Since he was a photographer, he said he knew all the ins and outs of the business. He told me he was looking to start his own agency and I was his first recruit. Of course, I naïvely fell for his charms. And I hoped it would lead me to you, Olive. That day, I wrote Momma a letter and packed a bag. Since I was eighteen, she couldn't stop me anyway.

"But once we arrived at his apartment, I quickly realized I had fallen into some sort of trap. Things seemed off. At first, he took me to a couple of shoots and I thought he might be legit. But one night, after too much drinking, he came into my room and —" She started to choke.

"Opal, it's okay. I know what you mean," I coaxed.

"Anyway, it was while he was taking me that I noticed your name tattooed across his chest. It was then that I knew. I was a pawn in some sick game. For weeks, he did sadistic things to me. Tonight, he fell asleep and happened to leave his phone on the bedside table within reach. I called Momma and begged her for your phone number. At first, she demanded I come home and refused to give it to me. When I told her I was tied to a bed, she finally conceded. And now I am here. The only good thing about this is I'm here with you now, Olive."

I kissed her cheek. "Opal, you're safe now and you're here with me. Things can only get better."

Chapter TWENTY -ONE

Bray

BETWEEN MY MOTHER being a bitch to Olive and having to rescue Opal from Drake, last night had been a night from hell. Olive had spent the night with Opal. The two had been glued to the hip this morning when I left for work.

"Bray," Jordan boomed as he walked into my office and plopped down.

I pulled myself from my thoughts of the events of last night and looked up at him. "What's up, Jordan?" I asked.

He grinned at me and dropped a pamphlet on my desk. I picked it up and look at him in confusion. The pamphlet was for The Stratosphere in Las Vegas.

I looked up at him questioningly. "What's this?"

"Elizabeth said, and I quote, 'There will be no fucking bachelor party.' And since I love my woman, I will agree to her wishes. But things have been hectic for all of us here at work, and with the wedding coming up next month, I thought we could all use a break. I've reserved rooms there for all of us this upcoming weekend. Please tell me you don't have plans."

This was the last thing I wanted to do—spend time with Pepper while she was pissed at Olive and me.

"Uh, Jordan, I don't know if that's such a good idea. Pepper is pretty angry with me and Olive right now. This seems like a disaster waiting to happen."

"What do you mean? Why would she be upset with you? She never mentioned anything to me."

"Olive and I are together now. She found out and was super pissed—even going as far as to kicking Olive out of the apartment. I'm sorry, man, but I just don't think it's a good idea."

"Wait, what? She kicked her out?" he asked angrily.

Well, shit. I hesitantly nodded in confirmation. He reached into his pocket and retrieved his phone. Moments later, he had her on the phone.

"Hey, babe. How's work going today?" he asked through clenched teeth.

After she stated her response, he cut right to the chase.

"Did you have a fight with Olive?" After a few quiet moments, he spoke again. "I see."

I could hear her frantically trying to explain herself on the other end.

"I get why you're upset, but you need to fix this. We're going out of town this weekend. Everyone's going, and I hope that you can work this out with Olive. Love you," he said and hung up. I'd never seen those two fight, so it was awkward to be a part of that conversation. After all that, there would be no way I could tell him no now.

"When do we leave?" I asked, resigned to going on the trip. I would love it if Olive and Pepper could make up. It would be one less thing to worry about.

"Friday morning. I'll send you the information so you can book flights for you and Olive. But don't worry. I've already booked the rooms," he grinned at me, his mood from moments earlier having dissipated.

"Add one more room. I'm sure Olive is going to want her

sister to come with us."

Jordan beamed at me as he stood. "On it," he said before leaving.

I sighed and dialed Olive to tell her the newest developments. When her phone went straight to voicemail, I had a nervous feeling about it. A few minutes later, I tried again. Not taking any chances, I grabbed my keys and hauled ass out of my office and ran right smack into Andi. She would have toppled over had I not grabbed her elbows and held her steady. Of course Jackson would choose that moment to walk out of his office.

He glared over at where my hands held on to Andi. I didn't have time for his stupid jealous shit today—Olive wasn't answering and it worried me sick.

"Not now, Jackson," I shot out over to him as I released Andi. "Olive hasn't answered my calls and it doesn't sit right with me after last night."

Jackson's features quickly morphed into concern. "You think she's okay? Do I need to come with you?"

"Nah, I'm sure she's fine, but I will feel better once I talk to her. I'll text you and let you know," I called out over my shoulder as I made my way to the elevators.

Fifteen minutes later, I was pounding away on the button to the elevator in my own building to no avail. For some reason, the wiring acted up from time to time, and building maintenance couldn't figure out why. Sighing in frustration, I pushed through the stairwell door and took two steps at a time until I made it to the third floor. I quickly slid the key into the door and breathed a sigh of relief when I saw Olive standing on a stepladder, washing the big panoramic windows. Her ass was sexy as hell in her short pink shorts. It jiggled each time she swiped the cloth across the glass. My cock sprang to life as I thought of her bent over before me while I pounded her from behind.

Wait—what?

"Olive!" I shouted at her once I'd snapped out of my day-dream.

She jumped, startled, and nearly fell off the ladder. "You scared me!" she squeaked out as she climbed down.

"What were you thinking? You shouldn't be climbing ladders while pregnant! And furthermore, why weren't you answering your phone?" I demanded angrily. I was upset from the stress of everything and unfairly taking it out on her. My jaw was uncontrollably clenching as I seethed in anger.

Her brow furrowed as she glared at me. Stomping over to me, she stopped right before our chests touched. "Why don't you try again?" she hissed.

I could tell she was pissed, and with good reason. I'd just burst into the apartment like a lunatic. Her eyes were filled with fire as we had a stare down.

"Where's your sister?" *Another demand.*

She licked her lips before she spoke again, and that's when I lost my fire. It was quickly replaced by hunger—for her. Seeing her all worked up and standing her ground had done something to my heart. She wasn't the nervous, scared woman she had been months ago when we first met. This girl was coming into her own, and I loved it. It was in that moment that I realized I truly loved her and had for some time.

"She's napping. And I turned off my phone," she finally answered. Nervousness briefly passed over her features.

Grasping on to her hips, I pulled her to me. Once her body was pressed against mine, she could feel my arousal plain as day. Now the fire had left her eyes as well. Leaning down, I captured her mouth with mine and tasted her plump bottom lip. Her eyes fluttered closed and she moaned into my mouth.

Pulling away, I looked at her again. "Olive, I was worried. I'm sorry I yelled at you."

She snaked her arms around my neck to hug me. I pulled her

close and squeezed her tight. My hands slid down her back and found what they were looking for, grabbing a handful of each ass cheek.

"Fuck me, Olive. Now." *Another demand.*

Her answer was to hop up and wrap her legs around my waist. Not wasting any time, I stalked into my room and shut the door behind us. Walking over to the bed, I set her back down on her feet. I knew being bossy with Olive probably wasn't the route to go with her, but I was still fired up about the last few days.

"Take your clothes off." *Demand.*

She didn't argue but held my gaze with her own sensual one. Latching on to the hem of her t-shirt, she yanked it over her head, revealing her two perky mounds, which seemed to look swollen today. She wasn't wearing a bra, which was incredibly hot. How I hadn't noticed that until now was beyond me.

Her thumbs found the waistband of her cotton shorts and she slid them down, along with her panties, to her ankles, giving me a full view of her recently developed sexier-than-hell curves. She still was pretty flat on her tummy, but I knew it would only be a matter of time before she would start to show.

Needing to touch her, I gently cupped each breast in my hands. While I fondled her, I kissed her deeply. When she whimpered, clearly turned on, I pulled away.

"I want to watch you touch yourself," I said gruffly. *Still a demanding tone.* I pulled away from her and started loosening my tie. She nodded and slid her hand down to her smooth pussy. Slipping a finger inside herself, she dragged the wetness from inside up her slit, locating her clit.

"Mmm," she moaned.

I yanked off my tie and set to unbuttoning my shirt while I watched her touch herself.

"That's it, baby. Go faster," I urged while I shrugged out of my shirt.

She'd already closed her eyes, and her free hand had found her nipple, which she lazily rubbed.

"Make yourself come, baby, because as soon as you do, I'm going to fuck you so hard," I growled. Again, she nodded and picked up her rhythm. Her breaths were becoming short and ragged. Unbuckling my slacks, I slid them and my boxer briefs to the floor, stepping from them.

"Oh," she panted, signaling the beginning of her orgasm. Her finger furiously stroked her clit as she got closer.

"That's it, Olive," I crooned, stepping right up to her so that we were inches apart. She panted heavily. Leaning over, I sucked on her neck for a second and then just pressed my lips against her. "I want you to come for me now, baby." *Demand.* I sucked her back into my mouth and gently sank my teeth into her flesh, successfully sending her over the edge.

"Bray!" she groaned as a shudder tore through her body. When she finally stopped convulsing, I grabbed her wrist and pulled it up to my mouth. Finding her wet finger, I dragged between my lips, tasting her essence. After I licked it clean, I grinned at her.

"Now we're going to fuck," I informed her as I spun her around. My cock pressed between her ass crack as my hands roamed her body.

She whimpered when one found her breast and the other her clit. Both were swollen and sexy as hell.

"Climb onto the bed and get on your knees and elbows. I want to see your beautiful ass pointed up for me. I need to caress it while I pound your pussy." *Another demand.*

When she ignored me, really enjoying the circular pattern I'd created on her clit, I pulled it away and playfully popped her on the ass. She sighed in frustration but obliged by climbing onto the bed. Once she was in the requested position, I climbed up behind her. Grabbing both of her perfect ass cheeks in my hands, I gave them a little squeeze.

I slipped a finger into her wet pussy and stroked her lazily. She must have wanted more speed because she kept pointing her ass closer to me. Finally, I pulled my finger from her to give her what she really wanted.

"You want me to fuck you, baby?" I asked huskily.

"Yes, please," she begged, her voice barely above a whisper.

Grabbing ahold of my throbbing cock, I teased her wet opening. "Baby, you can do better than that. Talk dirty to your man. You want me to fuck you?" I asked as I continued to stroke my dick against her, not making any moves to push it inside.

She whimpered in need. "Bray, I need you to f—I need you to fuck me. Hard," she choked out. She hardly ever cussed, so it was naughty to hear it coming from her lips.

"Tell me again," I demanded.

"Fuck me hard!" she cried out.

I pushed myself deep inside her until I was as far as I could go. Her body throbbed around me and I took a second to gather my bearings so I didn't come right away. Our dirty talk really had me turned on.

Grabbing on to her hips, I began thrusting hard, enjoying the sound of my body slapping her ass. Each time I slammed into her, my balls would slap her pussy lips, creating a hot fucking sensation. It wouldn't be long before I came, so I reached a hand around her and found her clit. Stroking it quickly in a pattern I knew she loved, I tried desperately not to come until she had reached her own orgasm.

With my free hand, I gripped her ass again before sliding my thumb between her cheeks. I'd barely stroked her puckered hole when I felt her come. Her pussy clenched my dick and pulled out my own orgasm instantly. I thrust several more times until the last of my come was inside her.

She sighed in contentment. "Bray, that was amazing," she purred and pulled herself off my cock. She collapsed onto the bed, still breathing heavily.

I stretched out beside her and stroked her back. "Come here." *Another demand.*

She looked up and grinned at me, looking very much like a sexy vixen in her glow that was part 'just fucked' and part pregnant. Stretching one of her long legs across me, she straddled me and laid her body on my chest. The wetness that dripped from her body on to my stomach had my dick coming back to life. Her fingers threaded their way through my hair, and she kissed me deeply on the lips. The way she looked at me in that moment made my heart swell happily. *I love you.* That was my thought, but for some reason, I didn't voice it. Instead, I nudged her with my now hard cock.

"Make love to me." *My final demand.*

Chapter TWENTY-TWO

Olive

"BRAY, OH MY GOSH! Check out this bathroom," I called out to him. He was still telling me all about the contents of the mini fridge in the room.

"That tiny bottle of vodka is thirty-nine bucks," he whistled in awe.

Jordan had spared no expense in these rooms. They were all fancy suites, including Opal's. Bray walked into the bathroom and smiled. We were both in awe at the sheer luxurious feel of it.

"I want you in that Jacuzzi tonight," he said in the demanding tone we'd recently found was hot for the both of us.

"Well, I read that it is okay to take baths while pregnant, but they just shouldn't be too hot. As long as we keep it a nice warm temperature, we should be f—" I replied before getting interrupted by a chaste kiss on my lips that instantly warmed my insides.

"I read it too, baby. I'll take care of you. You know that."

And I did know that. Bray had been taking care of me since the day we met. He took care of all of my needs—emotionally and physically. Bray meant the world to me.

"Are you ready to head down for dinner?" he asked.

I frowned because I really wasn't ready. This was the first time I would see Pepper since the incident of her kicking me out. She still didn't know I was pregnant. It was going to be beyond awkward, but I'd promised Bray I would try for Jordan's and Andi's sakes. I still loved Pepper, so I wanted us to get past our issues.

"Ready as I'll ever be," I sighed. He kissed the top of my hand and led me out of the bathroom.

On the way downstairs, we knocked on Opal's door. When she answered, we giggled when we saw one another. The last few days, we'd been practically inseparable. It was so good to have my sister back. She looked great now too. Thankfully we were close to the same size so she was able to wear my clothes. Since she'd come to us with nothing, we'd had to improvise. She was the same little sister I remembered from living back home, but now she was a beautiful woman. It was hardly noticeable that just days ago she had been tied to a bed, having unmentionable things being done to her by Drake.

"Are you ready, Opal?" I asked. She nodded and we all headed down the hallway.

Bray, always needing to touch me, had his hand on the small of my back, guiding me toward the elevators.

"I can't wait to meet your friends under better circumstances. I'm so embarrassed that Jackson and Bray saw me naked that night. I didn't speak two words to Andi. It will be nice to hang out like normal people," she said.

I laughed and pulled her in for a side hug. "I wouldn't say we're norm—"

We were interrupted by the elevator doors opening, which greeted us with a very hot and heavy Jackson and Andi. With a smug grin over at us, he slowly withdrew his hand from under her dress. She was flushed but looked horrified.

"Olive, Bray, Opal!" she shrieked in surprise.

"Whoa, Fifty Shades much?" Opal laughed.

"Get a room," Bray teased as we joined them on the elevator. He squeezed my hand and pecked my cheek.

"Where are Jordan and Pepper?" I asked, trying to change the subject for Andi's sake.

"They're going to meet us in the restaurant at seven. How are you feeling, Opal?" she questioned my sister.

"I'm great, and it's awesome to finally meet you both under more normal circumstances."

The elevator doors opened to the floor of the restaurant and we all shuffled out. Jordan and Pepper were waiting by the entrance. He waved at us but her back was still turned. I suddenly felt sick to my stomach at having to speak to her again.

"Hey, guys!" Jordan greeted happily when we reached them. Pepper turned and smiled at Andi but refused to look at anyone else. My heart sank.

"Pepper, meet Olive's sister, Opal," Andi politely introduced.

Pepper arched an eyebrow as she looked at my sister in a non-friendly manner. She nodded once and turned her back to us. Opal hissed out an, "Oh no she didn't," from beside me.

"Elizabeth! You're being rude," Jordan growled through clenched teeth.

"I'm confused. Is your name Elizabeth or Pepper?" my sister chimed up from beside me. My body tensed as I realized it was her way of standing up for the both of us. Opal was a smart cookie and probably sensed the animosity.

Pepper spun back around and glared at her. Jordan grabbed ahold of her arm and whispered a warning under his breath.

"The people who love me call me Elizabeth. *You* can call me Pepper," she spat out at my sister before turning and storming into the restaurant.

That stung.

While Jordan always called her Elizabeth and Andi mostly remembered, the rest of us still called her Pepper.

"Everything's going to be okay, baby," Bray whispered into my ear as we followed her inside.

We managed to make it through dinner without incident. Pepper directed all of her conversation toward Andi. Thankfully Jordan made sure to include everyone else. He even had us all laughing most of the time. Several times, Pepper made sure to glare hatefully at me. When Bray kissed my cheek at one point, she slammed her fork down.

"I can't take this anymore," she huffed out, pinning me with her stare.

My eyes widened as I looked over at Bray from the corner of my eye. He was just shaking his head, trying desperately to refrain from going off on her.

"Take what, Pepper? Andi fucking knows. You're the only one being a bitch here," he snarled back at her.

She snapped her head to Andi, who looked back at her guiltily.

"You *know* and you're okay with it?" she demanded.

"Uh, yeah. They told me the other day. Look, hon. We were waiting until we were all here together to talk it out with you—to smooth things over. We're all best friends, and there isn't a reason why we can't get past this. I promise I'm okay with it. You should be too," Andi said reassuringly.

The table was silent as Pepper processed her words. Her glare softened to a frown and a tear escaped.

"Andi, I was so worried about what it would do to you. You nearly killed the both of us back then. I couldn't go through that again," she whispered. Jordan reached over and clutched her hand. I felt my own eyes fill with tears.

"I know. Thanks for looking out for me, babe. But we want Olive to be happy too. They're happy, Pepper."

Pepper risked another glance in my direction. The sadness on her face reflected the memories she had of when Andi had nearly died. I felt my heart break open. Recovering from the vulnerable look, she put on her Ice Queen face again and reached for her purse on the floor.

"If you all will excuse me. I'm going to my room for the night."

Andi stood quickly. "I'm going with you—so we can talk."

I finally spoke up. "Pepper, I'm sorry. I—"

"No. I'm not ready to talk about this right now, Olive. But heed my advice. Get as far away from *him* as you can. Once a cheater, always a cheater," she hissed at me. She and Andi started to leave when Jordan stood.

"Baby, let me pay the bill and I'll be up to the room," he said, trying to provide her some comfort.

I could hear Bray grinding his teeth furiously from beside me. He was scowling with his arms crossed across his chest when I looked over at him. Jackson was staying out of it by typing on his phone. Opal was studying the hem of her shirt obviously, feeling as uncomfortable as the rest of us.

"No, Jordan. Hang out with your brother. I'll be fine. Talk to you later," she assured before kissing his cheek and leaving with Andi.

"Well that was fucking awkward as hell," Jackson grunted, not looking up from his phone.

"Bray, I don't feel so well. I'm going to go on up as well," I told him. And I felt really nauseated. Probably a little of both pregnancy and Pepper.

"Okay, let's go," he huffed, still clearly very angry with her for lashing out at me.

"No, I think you guys should go have some drinks or something. Opal can go with me. There's no need for all the women to spoil all the fun tonight," I told him shakily. If I kept up with these nauseous dizzy spells, I would need to call the doctor. It was really putting a damper on my everyday life.

He nodded as I kissed his forehead. Before I got too far away, he grabbed my hand and pulled me back to him.

"Come here," he whispered. When I leaned in closer, he softly said, "I lo—I'll text you later."

Pecking him on the forehead one last time, I left with Opal.

Chapter TWENTY-THREE

Bray

THIRTY MINUTES LATER, the three of us guys were sitting at one of the casino bars, finally relaxing after several shots of Patrón.

"Oh, shit, Jordan. I forgot to tell you that I'm going to be meeting with one of Mr. Higgins's hotel friends. He wants to purchase an existing building and do a teardown. It could be a huge account if I take it," I told Jordan.

He grinned and slapped my shoulder. "That's awesome, Bray. You've really helped land us some big accounts—helped save the company really. We know it wasn't Jackson's lazy ass," he joked.

Jackson looked up from his phone and flipped us off. "Whatever, dickheads," he grumbled.

Jordan and I laughed as the cocktail waitress come up to us.

"Hi, I'm Candy. We just had a shift change, so I can help you if you need anything," she purred as she batted her eyelashes at us. Her tits were spilling out of the top of her uniform, making it very awkward to look at her.

"Candy, bring us another round. We're enjoying one last weekend of debauchery before I get married next month," Jordan told her jovially. That guy was always grinning like a fool.

"Oooh, so like a bachelor's party weekend?" she asked, once again batting her long eyelashes at him.

"Something like that. The women are with us, but they're in the rooms."

"Ahhh, I see. Well, there's a private party happening right now on level eight at the pool. Someone told me Nikki Sixx was going to be there. It's by invite-only but I could get you access," she flirted. Jordan was oblivious to the fact that she was pushing her tits closer to his face.

"Candy, that sounds great! Bring us two more shots of Patrón each and there'll be a nice tip waiting for you," he instructed, grinning at her. She winked at him and sauntered off to the bar. The poor girl probably thought he was flirting with her, but I knew better. Jordan only had eyes for Pepper, and he was fucking friendly as hell. People mistook that for flirting all the time.

After two more shots and a funny-as-hell wrestling match between Jordan and Jackson in the elevator, we finally made it to the pool party. Rock music blasted as soon as we got off the elevator. People were everywhere, dancing and drinking. We were still taking in the scene when a group of people got up and abandoned a table near the bar. Jackson and I snagged it while Jordan took off to get us more drinks.

"Dude, I still can't believe you knocked up Olive," Jackson laughed. He was a lot friendlier as a drunk motherfucker.

"I'm glad it happened. I love her. She doesn't know it yet, but I do," I told him honestly.

His face sobered up and he slapped my knee. "She knows. How can she not? You two have been glued to each other's sides since Andi's birthday party. You're growing on me, Bray—I'm starting to like you. But you better not fucking prove me wrong or I'll beat the living shit out of you," he threatened.

I nodded, agreeing that I wouldn't ever hurt her.

"Who's going to beat the shit out of whom?" asked Jordan, nearly spilling all the contents of the drinks as he clumsily set them down on the table.

"You're fucked up, dude," Jackson laughed at him as he grabbed the fullest of the three drinks.

"I'm not fucked up, I'm fucking happy," Jordan grinned over at him.

"Hey, boys. Looking for some company?" a female voice purred.

The three of us looked up to see four women scantily clad in barely there bikinis. Makeup was perfect and hair was in place. They even had fucking high heels on. Who wore high heels to the pool?

"Nope. We're just fine having a guys' night," I told her as I refrained from looking at her shoes again. I mean, really. Who wore fucking high heels to the pool?

"Are you gay? All the hot ones are gay. I bet we'd turn you straight given the chance," she purred.

"I see Nikki Sixx," Jackson said, pointing off toward a group of people. The girls snapped their heads in that direction and pranced off without even a goodbye.

"Fucking groupies," I laughed. I downed the rest of my drink and started to feel really tired. A little rest of the eyes seemed to be in order.

"Wake up, fucker," Jackson chuckled and kicked my knee.

I snapped my eyes open. "How long was I out?" I asked as I wiped drool from the corner of my mouth. "And where's Jordan?"

"Pepper has him pussy-whipped. He left not long after you passed out. You've been out for at least thirty minutes. Check your phone, stupid-ass. I sent you a text."

I rubbed my eyes and pulled out my phone. When I realized I had several texts, my heart rate picked up. I hoped Olive was okay. The most recent text was from Jordan, so I read it first.

Jordan: Fix it, dickhead.

Um, okay? Drunk-ass. The next one was from an unknown number.

Unknown: It's Pepper. You're a stupid-ass mother-fucking asshole. I hate your guts and I hope you rot in hell. When I see you again, I'm going to cut off your balls and shove them down your throat. Stupid fucker.

What in the hell was wrong with that woman? She was seriously obsessed with terrorizing me about that one fucking time in my life when I'd hurt Andi. Clearly she was the only person who didn't have a forgiving bone in her body. The next text was from Andi.

Andi: Bray, you need help. What is wrong with you?

Okay, so I was clearly missing something here. I looked up at Jackson, but he had his eyes closed now. I scrolled on to the next text, which happened to be from Olive. My heart pounded furiously when I read it.

Olive: I trusted you. You told me I could trust you and I believed you. Don't ever talk to me again.

What the fuck? Was I so drunk that I was missing the point here? Why was Olive so upset with me? When I pulled up the last text, I nearly dropped my phone. It was from that stupid sleeping fucker across from me.

Jackson: Bray loves blow jobs.

The text wouldn't have been that bad, but it was the picture he'd sent me. The picture was of the four scantily clad bikini Barbies all posing around me. The ringleader had situated herself between my legs and was pretending to give me a blow job. The others had their tits pressed against me and one even had her tongue in my ear. No fucking way. And since my stupid ass had been passed out, my head was tilted back, looking like I was enjoying the whole fucking thing.

"I'm going to fucking kill you!" I roared at Jackson as I

sprang from my chair, lunging at him. His eyes flew open right before I punched him in the jaw.

"What the fuck man? It was a joke," he snapped, standing quickly to better defend himself.

"Are you trying to make everyone fucking hate me? Why would you send that picture to them? To her? Tell me fucking why!" I demanded. My fists were clenching on either side of me, ready to take another swing.

"I don't know what you're talking about. I just sent it to Jordan. It was a joke. See?" he said, retrieving his phone from his pocket. When he pulled it open, his eyes grew wide. "Shit! I sent it to my entire fucking address book!" he exclaimed, now checking his own texts.

I growled, "Fuck you," to him and stormed off toward the elevators. He quickly jogged after me and caught up right before the elevators opened.

"I'm sorry, man. Shit, I even sent that to Mom. I just got a nasty reply back from her. And Andi texted me a million times. Dammit! I can't believe I sent it to everyone. It was a joke for Jordan. I didn't mean to do this, Bray. You've got to believe me," he groaned as we entered the elevator.

"Well, everyone fucking hates me now," I spat out.

"We'll fix it. Andi will be pissed at me for doing it, but I will take the heat. You were passed out—I thought it would be funny as shit. I didn't think this would happen."

Once we got to our floor, I took off in a jog to our room. Finding my key, I slid it into the slot and went inside. It was empty—just like I'd thought. Going back out, I went next door to Opal's door. Jackson stood next to me, ready to defend my fucking honor.

"Olive, let me in," I demanded as I pounded on the door. I could hear a flurry of female voices—one familiar one was wailing. My stomach sank at hearing her so upset.

The door creaked open a few inches and a furious Pepper glared back at me. I tried to push it open but the chain was engaged, effectively stopping me.

"Pepper, let me see Olive. This is all a big understanding. Please—" I began.

"No, Bray. You can't see her. I can't believe you can't keep your dick in your pants for five minutes. Don't ever talk to my fucking friends ever again!" she screamed through the crack.

"Pepper, wait. It's my fault. I—" Jackson started to explain.

"Fuck you, Jackson! You took the fucking picture. What kind of friend does that make you to Olive?" she snapped. Not waiting for a response, she slammed the door back in my face and engaged the bolt lock.

I beat and kicked on the door while Jackson tried to reach Andi by phone. After several more minutes later of this, hotel security came storming down the hall toward us.

"Do we have a problem here?" one of the big burly men asked.

"Yes! My girlfriend thinks I cheated on her and won't let me in to explain!" I shouted in explanation.

"Sir, when people have been drinking, emotions get high. I'm going to have to ask you to go back to your room. You'll have to work this out in the morning when you're sober," he instructed calmly.

"But I fucking love her! I need to see her!" I argued.

"Tomorrow. End of story. Now go on before I have to ask you to leave the premises," he ordered.

Defeated, I slammed the door one last time with my palm and stalked back into my room, leaving Jackson to feel guilty about the shitstorm he'd started.

Chapter TWENTY-FOUR

Olive

GUTTED. I FELT like someone had climbed into my soul, dug their claws in, and shredded my joy on the way back out. *That someone is Bray.* I spent the entire night crying my eyes out. Distraught didn't even begin to cover how I felt after what he'd done.

Reluctantly, I opened my eyes. There was no way I wanted to face today. I just wanted to forget about it all. Especially him. The four of us girls had slept in a tangled mess of limbs in Opal's king-sized bed. Last night, after I'd heard Bray and Jackson begging for us to let them in, I'd completely lost it until I had cried myself to sleep.

Pepper had gone into mama-bear mode and fiercely protected me the best way she knew how—by not letting them in. Once I'd told her that I was also pregnant with Bray's baby, she'd been furious but she'd directed it at him—even offering for her and Jordan to help me out if things got rough. Pepper had also apologized for kicking me out and said that the apartment was there if I needed it. She was back to being the best friend I knew and loved.

Andi offered me empathy. She of all people knew exactly what I was feeling in that moment. Her sympathetic smiles had sent me into fitful hysterics every time. *How could I have been so stupid?* Pepper had warned me right out of the gate with Bray, yet I'd still chosen to blindly fall for him. Hadn't the stories of Andi's own horrific journey with Bray been enough? Why had I had to test it out to see if he'd actually changed—for me?

I could tell that Opal wanted me to hear Bray out. Every time Pepper would go on a rant about him, she would roll her eyes. I knew my sister well enough to see when she was covering up her feelings. And her stance was that I needed to talk to him. I just didn't know if I could do that without breaking completely in half.

Sandwiched between Pepper and Andi, I quietly tried to ease myself out of bed without waking them. It had to only be like five or six in the morning, which meant that hopefully I wouldn't wake anyone. My stomach roiled, and I knew I had a sleeve of crackers in my bag next door. There was no way I wanted to see him, but I needed those crackers before I made myself sick. By sneaking over there this early in the morning, I would be able to also grab my bag since Bray would be passed out. He clearly had been wasted last night—not that it was an excuse for him to cheat on me.

The girls were still asleep so I was able to easily slip out of the room undetected. Very quietly, I put the keycard in and un-locked the door to the room next door with a beep that had me cringing. Ever so softly, I eased the door open and slipped inside. The room was dark, as the blackout curtains were drawn. Stealth-ily, I inched my way into the room and fumbled along to the area where I remembered leaving my bag. Kneeling down, I unzipped the zipper and felt inside to make sure the crackers were still in-side. Once I'd made certain they were there, I slung the back over my shoulder and stood to leave. Instantly, I felt dizzy and light-headed, so I knelt back down in an effort to not faint. Defeated, I quietly opened my bag once more to pull out the crackers. Getting them open without making noise was a feat in itself. Finally though, I was able to sneak one out and began nibbling on it.

After a few minutes of regaining my bearings by eating half the sleeve of crackers, I felt well enough to make my escape. Soundlessly, I stuffed the crackers back into my bag and stood. I was just making my way back toward the door when I ran smack into Bray's familiar hard chest.

"Oh!" I squeaked out in surprise.

His unique scent sent chills that I fought viciously to ignore right down to my core. This man, who was supposed to love me, had cheated on me. Tears sprang in my eyes and angrily ran down my cheeks.

"Olive," he croaked out and wrapped his arms around me. My body disregarded the screams of my mind and my heart as it relaxed into him, so much so that my bag slid from my shoulder and hit the floor. *Thud!* Suddenly, I was snapped back into reality again.

"Don't touch me!" I hissed quietly at him. If the girls heard us shouting from next door, we'd have a big dramatic scene on our hands.

"Olive, please hear me out. You have no idea how wrong you have it," he pleaded with me. He'd unheeded my demand not to touch me because now his large hands were stroking my back as he pulled me into him.

I tried to push away, but I was enraptured in all that was Bray. My body was a traitor to me, and all I could do was inhale him as he hugged me. It wasn't until I heard him whispering soft assurances to me that I realized I was sobbing.

"Baby, please hear me out."

Ignoring his pleas but still a victim of my duplicitous hands, I slid my arms around his waist, needing to feel closer to him. I buried my face into his chest and attempted to block out everything.

One of his hands came around between us and splayed out

over my stomach. Again, I felt gutted at the realization that this man, the father of my child, had been unfaithful to me. A mournful sob escaped me. His strong hands gripped my hair and pulled, tilting my head up to his. It was dark, so I couldn't see his face. I didn't need to see him though.

Everything about him was seared into my memory.

Into my mind.

Into my heart.

Softly, he pressed kisses all over my face as if he could kiss away my pain. His lips finally found my own, and I whimpered when he softly sucked my bottom lip into his mouth. My mind spun as I felt him slowly guide us to the bed. What was I doing? Why wasn't I screaming at him?

When the backs of my legs hit the bed, he broke his kisses to pull off his shirt. My hand immediately moved up to his chest, where I greedily caressed him. Why was I so desperate to touch him? I had a feeling it would be the last time, and my heart was shattering at that notion. Tears fell silently as I stroked the grooves of his muscled abdomen.

"It isn't what you think," he murmured into my ear as he grabbed hold of the hem of my dress. Very efficiently, he pulled it off my body in one swift motion. I felt his hands work the clasp of my bra, and seconds later, he tossed it to the floor. The chill of the air immediately hardened my nipples.

Finding my voice, I asked the question I desperately needed the answer to. "Why? How could you hurt me like that, Bray?"

Large hands skittered over my body, making me shudder with need. One found my breast while the other made its way up to my cheek, where it stroked me lovingly. The tenderness was almost too much to bear.

"Baby, I would never hurt you. Please just listen to me. Let me hold you and we can talk," he begged.

A huge part of me wanted to refuse him, but the part of me

that still cared deeply for him thought that was a great idea. His fingers were still threaded in my hair when I nodded. He exhaled loudly in relief before pecking my lips. Both of his hands found the tops of my panties and pushed them down my legs. He stepped back a bit to undo his pants, and within seconds, he was pressing his naked flesh against mine.

"Come on. Climb into bed. I need to hold you." His words were more of a command than a plea, but I complied nonetheless.

Finding the top of the covers, I drew them back and slid underneath them. His soft footsteps padded around the bed and he climbed in beside me. My body shivered as he pulled me over to him.

"We were drunk," he began softly. My heart seized sadly as I prepared myself for his tale. "I passed out and awoke to that fucker laughing his ass off," he growled at the memory. "He had called over some girls to pose like they were giving me a good time and snapped a picture. What was supposed to only go to his brother went out to his entire address book."

Thump.

My heart thudded to life as I tried to process his words.

Thump, thump.

"Last night I tried to tell you, but Pepper wouldn't let us in."

Thump, thump, thump.

His fingers once again found my belly, and my heart soared.

Thump, thump, thump, thump.

"Olive, I would never hurt you. You have to believe me. I love you, babe. I love our little A.B. too."

Now my heart was thumping happily with life. This was all just one unhappy misunderstanding.

"Why should I believe this?" I ask sadly.

"You just have to trust me, Olive. I've never given you any reason not to."

"Bray," I whispered tearfully.

His lips were on my face, rapidly kissing every inch of me. When he positioned himself over me to gain better access, I spread my legs and wrapped them around his hips. He must have needed me as much as I needed him because seconds later he had entered me with one quick thrust. We both groaned in relief and pleasure. Now that we were joined, he kissed me deeply, almost lazily.

"I'll never let you go, Olive. Last night was pure hell thinking I'd lost you. When you came into my room this morning, I knew it was my only shot to make things right. I love you so fucking much."

Threading my fingers through his hair, I brought his face back to mine and chastely kissed his lips.

"I love you too, Bray. Now make love to me."

Not needing to be told twice, he began thrusting into me, and since our emotions were running high, it only took a couple of those before we both unraveled with our orgasms.

Chapter TWENTY-FIVE

Bray

OLIVE WAS HERE. Safely curled in my arms. Fate had given me a chance this time and I'd taken it. She'd already fallen back asleep, so I took the moment to appreciate all that was her. My hand made its way to her barely swollen belly. It was beginning to grow, and I couldn't help the grin that spread over my face. My baby was inside. *Our baby.*

When my fingers came in contact with one of her scars, my euphoria dissipated as anger crashed into me. That fucker Drake was still out there. He'd not only hurt my gorgeous girl, but he'd hurt her sister too. I would find a way to get him put away. Surely these weren't the only two women he'd done this to. I was going to start investigating him once we got back from Vegas. There would be no way I would feel safe with him always out there looking for Olive. At least I knew where he lived now so that I could properly stalk him.

Sliding my hand up to one of her breasts, I gently fondled it. Her normally smaller, perkier tits had already started to grow larger with her pregnancy. My lips found her neck and I kissed her softly. She was perfect, and I'd die before I ever let anything happen to her.

"Morning," she said sweetly.

I kissed her down her neck and all the way to her breast, tenderly sucking it into my mouth.

"Oh," she gasped. Her hands immediately found my hair and I smiled against her flesh.

Leisurely, my free hand crept down to her smooth pussy. She exhaled loudly when my finger found her clit. Once I began a rhythm she loved, her hips met my movements. Within minutes, she was ripping the hair from my head as she screamed out my name in pleasure.

"I'm hungry," I teased, trying to hide the grin from my voice.

Still gasping for air, she agreed, "Me too."

In one fluid motion, I had her legs spread with my face between them.

"Bray!" she moaned when my tongue dragged along her slit.

Using my thumbs, I spread her open for me and feasted on the woman I loved. I sucked and licked her aggressively, wanting to draw out another orgasm from her. When I slid two fingers inside her very wet body, she gasped loudly. A few thrusts in her while I devoured her and she unraveled beneath me.

Pulling my fingers from her, I kissed one of her thighs all the way down to her knee. I skimmed my hands along the outside of her legs, making their way to her hips, where they gripped her fiercely.

"Make love to me, baby," she breathed.

"Your wish is my command," I teased, grinning when it awarded me a giggle from her.

Grabbing my cock, I pushed myself easily into her. All laughter subsided as she dug her heels into my back, urging me to continue. Leaning forward, I captured her mouth with mine and our tongues greedily tasted each other as I continued my plunging deep inside her.

Deep in my belly, I could feel the tightening of my climax as it made its way to my balls. Her own release was made known as her body trembled beneath me, which, in turn, sent me over the edge. Hot come filled her up as I rode out the last of my blissful shudders.

"Fuck, Olive. You always feel so good," I praised, still panting. Kissing her gently on the lips, I pulled out of her and climbed off the bed. "Come on, beautiful. Let's get showered. My baby needs breakfast. Daddy messed up and had dessert first," I laughed.

She giggled and followed after me.

Bang! Bang! Bang!

Someone was pounding on the door, and I had a niggling feeling that Bitch Pepper would be waiting for me on the other side. Olive hurried and threw on a clean dress. I didn't even bother putting on a shirt and just answered the door in my jeans, still dripping with water.

Andi was on the other side, quickly diverting her eyes as to not look at my half-naked form. Jackson of course was beside her and tossed me a nasty look. Flipping him off, I motioned for them to come in while I located a shirt.

"Olive, um, I brought Jackson over so he could explain what happened. It was just a misunderstanding. But from the looks of it, I guess you two already figured that out?" she asked, still unsure.

"Yes. Thank you though, sweetie," Olive acknowledged. They squeezed each other in a quick embrace and sat down on the bed.

"Well, now that we got that fucking shit sorted out. What's on the agenda today?" Jackson asked, stuffing his hands into his jean pockets.

"I don't care what we do, but I'm not leaving her side," I confirmed, glancing over in Olive's direction.

"I should probably go next door and tell Opal the game plan, whatever we decide. Where are Pepper and Jordan?" Olive asked Andi.

Andi frowned before replying, "I'm not sure what was going on. Pepper said she wasn't feeling well and set off to find Jordan this morning. She was acting strange and hasn't responded to my texts."

"Don't worry, baby. I'm sure Pepper will be back to her usual bitchy self by the time we meet up again. She never disappoints," Jackson teased.

When I couldn't hold back my laughter, Olive threw a pillow at me.

"What? It's true!" I chuckled, and Jackson joined in.

Another knock on the door.

Jackson sidestepped over and opened the door to the rest of our group. Opal hurried in and hugged Olive. The three girls were a flurry of voices as Olive explained the misunderstanding. Pepper stormed into the room and first punched Jackson hard in the gut.

"What the fuck, Pepper?" he gasped as he doubled over, trying to catch his breath. I was already laughing my ass off when I too got a punch to the gut. Just as I was about to tell her to go to hell, she burst into tears.

"Pepper! It's okay! It was all a misunderstanding!" Olive cried and rushed over to her, pulling her in for an embrace.

Jordan stalked over to her and stroked her hair while the girls hugged. His face was pensive. Breaking the drama that was our group since the moment we'd arrived in Vegas, Andi stood and cleared her throat.

"Okay, the spectacle ends now. We're all in fucking Vegas and we've spent all our time arguing and crying. From here on out, we're going to gamble, eat, and shop!" she exclaimed, clapping her hands. Andi always knew how to turn around an awkward situation. I threw her an encouraging look and grabbed my wallet from the dresser.

Stuffing it in my jeans, I grinned at her. "Lead the way, Blondie."

Chapter TWENTY-SIX

Olive

WE SPENT THE entire day sightseeing and gambling. The city was so big, and we'd barely scratched the surface. My feet were starting to swell, and I found myself looking for a place to sit at each casino we visited. Everyone was laughing and joking over at the bar, so Pepper and I found a bench and sat down. She'd kept me company each time I had to sit.

"Are you feeling okay, Olive? Do you need something to drink? Do we need to get you back?" she asked in a nervous flurry.

After I answered all of her questions, I couldn't help but wonder what was going on in her mind. She seemed lost in thought.

"Everything okay, Pepper?" I asked softly. Her eyes met mine and filled with tears. My heart pounded rapidly because something was definitely going on with her. She glanced nervously over at Jordan at the bar before looking back at me.

"How did you know you were pregnant?" she questioned in a whisper, once again peeking over at him. Things quickly clicked into place.

"Well, besides Bray suggesting I was, it was morning sickness. Right out of the gate. Pepper, do you think you might be pregnant?" I asked hopefully.

Her eyes met mine once again, and tears filled them. When her chin quivered, I quickly pulled her in for a hug.

"Pepper, what's going on? You know you can tell me anything," I urged.

She broke away and sniffled, nodding her head. "Olive, I think I may be pregnant but I don't understand how. I take my birth control every day. But recently, I feel ill all the time, my boobs hurt like a motherfucker"—she paused and we both giggled—"and my emotions are all over the place. I'm a mega bitch, more than usual, and I fucking cry at the drop of a hat!"

"Come on. Let's go," I said excitedly as I stood up, pulling her to her feet.

"Why? Where are we going?" she questioned.

"Hey, guys. We'll be right back!" I called to the group. Bray nodded and smiled at me as I half-dragged Pepper out of the casino.

"Shit, Olive! Where are you taking me?" she demanded once we were outside.

When she saw where we were headed, she put on the brakes, stopping me.

"No. No! Olive, I'm not ready. What if I am pregnant? What will Jordan do? We never talked about this!" Her voice was shrill, and she was close to having a panic attack right there on the sidewalk with people bustling by.

"Ignoring the inevitable won't help a thing, babe. We're going in there and buying a pregnancy test!" I informed her firmly as I once again led her into the drugstore.

"Olive, I'm so fucking scared. How will I be able to take care of a baby?" she whined as tears fell down her cheeks.

"If you are, then you'll do great. I just know it! Now let's get this done. Jordan is amazingly supportive. Together, you will be wonderful parents," I assured her as I grabbed a pregnancy test from the shelf.

After we bought the test, I went into the bathroom of the store with her. She was still pouting when I handed her the stick I had retrieved from the package.

"Here. Pee on it," I commanded.

"Shit, Olive. You're becoming quite sassy as a pregnant lady," she grumbled but took the test and walked into the stall. A few minutes later, she came out and set it on the counter beside the sink while she washed her hands.

After an impatient sigh, she asks, "Now fucking what?" she grumbled.

"Now we wait. Pepper, everything is going to be okay. No matter the outcome," I promised.

She finally smiled at me. "I just don't get it. How does this happen? I don't miss my pills. Ever."

I mulled it over, trying to figure out how she could indeed get pregnant while on the pill. Suddenly, the answer was as clear as day.

"Pep, when you had surgery on your wrist after the accident with Cole, didn't the incision get infected?" I asked, remembering her telling me about it.

"Yeah, but they gave me antibiotics and it cleared right u—" Her eyes grew wide as she figured it out. "Holy shit. Holy fucking shit, Olive. We never used another form of protection while I was on antibiotics. Motherfucker!" she exclaimed.

As she paced the room, I glanced over at the test. When she saw me looking, she couldn't help but glance at it as well. Abruptly, she dashed over to the test and picked it up.

"Congratulations, Momma," I told her softly, barely able to keep the excitement from my voice.

She turned to me with big tears in her eyes and smiled broadly. "I'm pregnant?" she asked in disbelief.

I nodded and hugged her tightly. "He's going to be excited,"

I promised.

"I hope so. I can't believe this, Olive. Me? A mom? Do they give you lessons for that shit somewhere?" she giggled through her sniffles.

"Girl, I don't know, but we better get signed up because I have no freaking idea what to do," I laughed.

She pulled away and grabbed a paper towel to wrap up the test. After she'd stuffed it into her purse, we walked hand in hand back to the casino bar, where our friends were waiting.

As soon as we entered the casino, we saw Jordan nervously waiting by the door.

"Elizabeth," he breathed in relief. I could see that he was worried sick about her as he hugged her.

When he pulled away, he frowned. "What's going on? Have you been crying?" he asked worriedly.

"Pepper, I'm going to go fin—" I began, but she interrupted me.

"No! Olive, please stay a minute," she begged.

Well, this was awkward. Poor Jordan looked like he was fretting that she was going to break up with him.

"Please, baby, tell me what's going on. You're killing me," he admitted quietly.

She withdrew the wadded-up paper towel from her purse and handed it to him.

"Jordan, I love you and I pray to God you're okay with this," she tearfully told him.

Confused, he took the wad from her. "What's this?"

"Just open it," I urged him.

He frowned at me and reluctantly opened it. Quickly, his frown dissolved and morphed into the huge grin we all knew and loved.

"Elizabeth, how?" he asked in disbelief, once again pulling her tight to him.

"Are you mad?" she cried into his chest.

"Fuck no! I'm so fucking happy I can't even stand it! I'm going to be a fucking dad!" he exclaimed happily. When she giggled, he turned and shouted to the entire casino, "My fiancée is pregnant! We're going to have a baby!"

Chapter TWENTY-SEVEN

Bray

"BABE, WE NEED to get up. We told them we'd meet them at the restaurant at seven," I whispered.

When she rolled over and pulled the pillow over her head, I chuckled. After all the walking we had done today, Olive was completely exhausted.

"If you're too tired, I'll text Jordan and tell him we're staying in. I'd love nothing more than to cuddle with you rather than get dressed up for dinner," I admitted.

Removing the pillow from her face, she smiled beautifully at me. "No, I'm just being a baby. I'm starving anyway."

Reaching over, I cupped her breast through her dress. Her nipple hardened at my touch. Both of her hands clutched my neck and brought me closer to her so she could kiss me. Sliding between her legs, I pressed my erection into her through my jeans.

"Bray," she moaned into my mouth as I continued to push it against her clit while we kissed. Her hands found my shirt and she hastily jerked it up my body. I pulled away momentarily and ripped it the rest of the way off before meeting her lips with mine again. This time, her fingers were at my jeans, efficiently undoing them and pulling my cock from the top of my boxers.

I pushed my jeans and boxers farther down my legs and positioned myself over her. Hooking her panties with my thumb and exposing her to me, I teased her wet entrance with my cock before slamming it all the way in.

"Oh God!" she wailed as I drove myself into her hard. Her hips met me thrust for thrust.

"Babe, you're so beautiful," I groaned. Digging my fingers into her hips, I fucked her wildly. She was the first to unravel, and she screamed my name as she dug her fingernails into my forearms.

"Fuck, I'm coming," she screamed. The moment her pussy clenched around my dick, I lost it and pumped my orgasm into her. Pulling out, I heaved myself on the bed beside her and started laughing hysterically. "What?" she demanded.

"You said 'fuck,'" I told her between laughs. "You never cuss, and when you do, that shit's funny."

"You're such a dork," she groaned and playfully punched me in the side.

"Oh my God, this salmon is to die for," Andi moaned as she polished off the last of her food. Olive giggled at her from beside me.

"Gross, Andi, quit talking about it. You're making me ill," Pepper complained. The poor girl, who'd I learned today was pregnant, had only ordered mashed potatoes. She said that everything else made her feel nauseated to even think about. The fact the Andi was making love to her food had Pepper looking green around the gills.

"Uh, guys," Jackson spoke up, gathering everyone's attention. He was white as a ghost. Quickly, he drained his wine glass and turned towards Andi, pulling both of her hands into his.

"Are you okay?" she asked, concerned.

"Yes, I uh—shit. I'm fine. Just listen," he grumbled. She nodded nervously, preparing herself for whatever he was about to tell her. "I have a confession," he began.

"So help me, Jackson, if you cheat—" Pepper snapped but was quickly cut off by Jackson.

"Cut the shit, Pepper. I'm trying to speak and you're not helping!" he growled at her.

"Jackie, cool the fuck off," Jordan warned as he pulled his napkin from his lap and tossed it on the table. He looked as if he were ready to take action if need be.

"Jesus! I'm trying to fucking talk here!" he griped.

"So talk, asshole," I barked. Whatever he was going to say to her seemed pretty bad by the way his skin had broken out into a sweat. Poor Andi looked close to tears. If he fucking broke up with her at the dinner table, so help me, I'd kill him. Olive squeezed my hand and threw me an uneasy glance.

"Go on. What is it?" Andi probed.

"Andi, I love you. You know that. I would never intentionally hurt you." The fact that he appeared nervous had everyone on edge. Jackson was always so self-assured, arrogant almost. His usual demeanor was gone, and that seemed to foreshadow bad news.

Andi snatched her wine glass and took a huge gulp before setting it back down on the table with shaky hands. My muscles were tense, ready to tackle Jackson if need be. He was already on my shit list from last night. If he hurt Andi tonight, he'd definitely be getting the smackdown he was more than owed.

He ran both hands through his hair in frustration as he tried to formulate the words he was going to say. "This is not at all going like I fucking planned."

His eyes skimmed the restaurant before landing on someone. He momentarily closed his eyes and drew in a deep breath.

"Andi, I fucking suck at this shit. I love you so much. My life was a damn joke until you walked into that bar prancing around like you owned the place and everyone in it. That moment I saw those long legs walk into that bar, I was hooked along with every other motherfucker there. But when you spoke with such confidence about your wants and needs, you fucking mesmerized me. In that moment that we shared in Ian's office, I knew you were different—knew I had to have you. Not just for the weekend, but for fucking ever. I may not be doing it in Central Park or Times Square, but none of that matters to me, and quite frankly, I know you well enough that you don't care either. All that is important to me is your answer. Baby, will you marry me?"

Andi gasped when Jackson pulled out a tiny jewelry box and retrieved a not-so-tiny platinum ring. He held it poised over her left finger but didn't attempt to put it on her.

"Do you remember that day I stood you up for our first real date? The day I saw you in the coffee shop?" he asked.

She nodded as a tear slipped out.

"That day, after Ian and I left, he went on home. I walked right into a fucking jewelry store and bought this ring. You fucking captivated me, Andi—you still do. When I got home, the rational side of me forced me to question what kind of psycho pansy buys an engagement ring for a woman he barely knows. But the fucking spellbound side of me remembered you sitting in the window with the sun shining in your blond hair. You were an angel to me that day. I knew—just fucking knew—I wanted you forever. Unfortunately, I was an idiot. A scared fucking idiot because I tossed the ring in the closet, told myself I was crazy for buying the damn thing, and stood you up for our date."

I quickly glanced around to see every single one of the girls at the table sniffling.

Jackson kissed the top of her hand before continuing. "Eventually, I knew no matter what, I'd never be able to live without you. I'd known it all along but didn't have the guts until now to tell you. Andi, please marry me. I promise to try hard to not be an asshole. Loving you is easy—not being an ass is a little tougher for me. But for you, I'll give anything a go."

Everyone chuckled, the mood of the group finally lightening once we realized this was his sad attempt at a proposal.

Pushing the chair out, he knelt down in front of her. "So what do you say? Will you marry me, Andi?" he asked, looking up at her. For someone who always had a smug ass look on his face, he sort of looked like a fucking lovesick puppy right now.

"Jackson, of course I'll marry you. I love you too," she answered, tears now freely falling down her cheeks. When I'd proposed to her, she hadn't cried. Guess we should have known at that point that we'd just been going through motions of what we'd thought was expected of us.

He slid the ring on her finger and wrapped his arms around her waist, resting his head in her lap, seemingly exhausted from his proposal. She stroked his hair lovingly. In that intimate moment, I realized just how much those two loved each other.

A squeal from a nearby table interrupted them and suddenly two female arms were wrapped around Andi.

"Trish?" Andi asked, turning to look at Jackson and Jordan's mom.

"Oh, sweetie. I'm so glad you said yes. It would have been real awkward if you chose another answer. George and I were almost at the point of backing out of the restaurant slowly since Jackson was clearly botching his proposal up so badly," she giggled as she brushed the hair away from Andi's eyes in a loving, motherly manner. I couldn't help but have the utmost respect for Trish in that moment. Andi's own mother was a distant bitch, and Andi had always been so desperate for motherly affection. Trish would clearly fill that void for her.

"I'm so glad that you were here for this, Trish, but I don't think you should have flown all the way out here for it. How long were you planning this?" she asked, turning back to Jackson, who was sitting back in his chair.

"Well, let's just say I have another surprise for you. I'm praying to God you will be okay with it," he told her, once again nervous.

"Baby, stop stressing. You know I love you. I trust you with my happiness—you know that," she reminded him.

He quickly kissed her lips and stood. "Okay everyone. Follow me," he announced, pulling Andi from her chair.

Ten minutes later, we were at the Chapel in the Clouds, where a minister ushered us inside as we arrived.

"Oh!" Andi gasped as she realized the engagement would be short-lived.

Twenty minutes later, we were congratulating Mr. and Mrs. Jackson Compton. The moment they said "I do," a weight had lifted. It was like I could finally breathe easy that she truly was happy.

Chapter TWENTY-EIGHT

Olive

IT HAD BEEN three weeks since Andi and Jackson's wedding. Everything seemed to be going smoothly. My doctor had prescribed some medicine to help with my nausea, which I quickly called Pepper and told her about. It was nice to chat with her about all things pregnancy related. Andi, probably a hundred times since Vegas, told us that she wanted to be pregnant with us. Jackson had given her the thumbs up for trying, and apparently that's all they'd been doing.

"You almost ready?" Opal called from Bray's living room. She was still staying in the guest room until she could get on her feet. Thankfully, Compton Enterprises was doing so well that they had promoted Andi to architect, which had been her goal all along, and hired Opal and two others as assistants. Jordan even told Opal that Compton Enterprises would pay for her education if she wanted to pursue a career in that field. She'd already gone online and completed her GED so that she could enroll at CUNY in the fall.

"Yep! Let me grab my coat," I told her as I came out of the bedroom. We were supposed to be meeting Bray over at his parents' house for dinner tonight. I was nearly sick with worry since this would be the first time seeing his mother again since our not-so-friendly meeting when we'd announced our pregnancy.

"Olive, it will be okay. She'll come around. I mean, come on. She can't be any worse than Momma," she joked. My heart sank even though it was the truth.

Our own mother didn't seem to care a bit about either of us. She was more concerned about what people would think about her. It was sad, really, that she would choose her friends over her family. I still hadn't told her I was expecting.

"You haven't met her. Connie is uppity and she hates me. I'll never compare to Andi in her eyes. To her, I am just a gold-digging female who got herself knocked up so she could be taken care of. What sucks is it seems sort of true considering I can't model while pregnant. Bray is so dead-set against me working or living anywhere else, but I can't help but feel like I'm living up to Connie's assumption of me," I confessed.

Opal frowned but came over and hugged me. "I'll be there to support you—as your family. If she knows what's good for her, she'll come around."

"I hope you're right."

My phone chimed, alerting me to a text. Thinking it was Bray, I quickly pulled it out to reply back to him.

Unknown: It took a while, but I found exactly where you are. Ollie, it's time you come home to me. You are, after all, my property. Check your stomach for confirmation. I believe I left my message loud and clear.

My legs buckled underneath me and I fell to my knees. *Drake.*

"Olive, so good to see you again," Connie greeted in a phony tone. I fought not to cry. Right now, I didn't have the energy to deal with her wrongfully hating me when there was a real threat out there to my baby and me.

"Connie, this is my sister, Opal. Opal, this is Bray's mom, Connie," I introduced. Even though I'd taken my nausea medicine, I still felt quite ill. Once Bray arrived, I would feel better.

The two women awkwardly shook hands. Afterwards, Connie led us from the entryway into the den, where an older man was sitting in a recliner, watching television.

"Jim, honey, our guests have arrived," she called out to him. Bray must have gotten his outgoing nature from Connie, because Jim just grunted his greeting and turned back to the television.

"Sorry, girls. Jim isn't that friendly. Please, come into the kitchen. I'll get you something to drink."

We followed her into the kitchen and sat at the barstools she motioned to. She politely talked about the weather as she fetched us each a bottle of water. My mind was elsewhere as I thought about what exactly Drake was capable of. I knew the man really knew no bounds when it came to me. The day I'd run into him and he'd seemed almost normal, I'd stupidly thought my worries were over. Then, after he'd hurt Opal and I'd realized he had been after me all along, my stomach had been in knots. But once again, he'd left me alone to the point where I'd conveniently pushed him from my mind and enjoyed my happy life with Bray.

"Olive?" Connie asked, pulling me from my thoughts. She was frowning at me. Clearly she had just asked me a question—one I hadn't even heard.

"Uh, yes?" I asked her, slightly distracted.

"I asked you if you planned on getting a job since modeling won't pan out for quite some time." She smiled, satisfied with her jab. God, this woman was ridiculous.

Refraining from rolling my eyes, because I simply wasn't in the mood for her games, I snippily told her, "I'm looking."

"Oh, darling, nobody will hire you in your condition," she

sweetly told me.

Opal snapped her head over to her. "Ma'am, with all due respect, I believe you're being quite horrible to my sister, whom doesn't at all deserve that treatment. Whatever problem you have with her, you need to bury in the past because she is carrying your family whether you like it or not. And if you have any hopes of being a part of that family, I suggest you check your attitude at the door and show her the respect that she—why, for the life of me, I can't understand—gives you," she suggested coolly.

Connie's jaw dropped as she flitted her glance between us.

"Hey, ladies," Bray greeted as he walked into the kitchen. Just being in his presence calmed me down tenfold. He kissed his mom's cheek before coming over to me and pulling me from the stool and into his arms. Once I was enveloped in his scent and protective arms, I broke down with loud sobs.

"Shh, Olive, it's okay. What's wrong, baby?" he asked softly as he held me tight.

"Oh crumbs! Olive, I'll try, okay? No sense in getting him to try and choose sides," Connie huffed from behind us.

"Jesus, lady! Her ex-boyfriend just texted her telling her that he's still stalking her and you've got it all twisted up that she's worried about your snooty ass. God, Olive, can we go already?" Opal griped, hopping off her stool. That girl had a mouth on her, which was what had surprised me the most when I found out she had gone off with Drake. She wasn't one who typically did well with being told what to do or how to act. But Drake was evil, controlling, and abusive. Even for a tough cookie like Opal, it would have been hard to be strong in his presence.

"Excuse me, little girl—" Connie started to snip out, but Bray cut her off.

"Wait a minute. Drake texted you?" Bray demanded, grabbing ahold of my shoulders and pulling me away to look at me.

Swiping the tears on my cheek away with the back of my

hand, I nodded. "He says he knows where I am and that it's time to take me home."

"Motherfucker!" he snarled. "Olive, baby, I will take care of you. He's not going to hurt you or our little A.B."

Thinking about the baby I had lost that fateful night when Drake carved his name into my flesh, I once again was overcome with sobs. Bray pulled me close and stroked my hair.

"Honey, what exactly did that man do to you? You seem terrified," Connie asked, all malice from her voice gone and replaced by motherly concern.

No longer afraid or ashamed of my body, I turned to her and lifted my shirt to reveal my barely swollen belly. When her eyes fell to the nasty messaged scarred across my stomach, she brought both hands to her mouth.

"Oh, you poor baby," Connie cried out and hurried over to me. She wrapped her arms around me and gave me a tight, comforting hug that I allowed myself to give in to. Those motherly hugs were hard to come by these days.

"Babe, we'll go to the police and tell them everything. I'm tired of you having to worry about him. We've got this little one to protect now," he told me and squeezed me tightly once again.

"Well, son, you're not leaving until you feed my grandbaby. But on the way home, please stop by the police station and make a report," Connie advised.

Three hours later, we crawled into Bray's bed, exhausted. The police had taken me seriously once I showed them my scarring. After some photographs for evidence, they'd promised they would proceed from their end by bringing in Drake for questioning and most likely booking him. They'd told us that if he didn't have any priors, he would most likely make bail and would be given a court date. I wasn't sure what good that would do except piss him off. We'd also filed a restraining order while we there. Hopefully by getting the police involved, he would stay away from me.

Now, we were lying curled up together after a hot shower, lost in our thoughts.

"What do you think he'll do?" I asked Bray. The question kept replaying in my mind. What lengths would he go to in order to get me back? Was this just a threat to try to scare or control me? Would he go as far as to kidnap me?

"He's not going to do anything so long as I have anything to do with it," he growled. I stretched my hand across his muscled chest and squeezed him. If there was a way to stay safely tucked under his arm for the rest of my life, I would never leave.

"I'm scared," I admitted, my voice barely a whisper.

He stroked my hair in an effort to comfort me. "I know, babe. Me too."

"My grandbaby needs these receiving blankets," Connie cooed as she held up a package of green-and-yellow-polka-dotted baby blankets. They really were quite adorable.

We were on our—at least—twentieth shopping trip since Connie and I had called out an unspoken truce the night Drake had texted me. At first, it'd been awkward, but after a few lunch dates and shopping trips, we were really growing close. Bray was extremely happy that Connie and I had gotten past our differences. It might have taken six months to get here, but she had eventually become someone I cared for deeply. I probably had Andi to thank for that one. After a lunch with the three of us and Andi gushing about being happily married, Connie had finally seemed to accept me as a suitable choice for her son.

"Connie, the baby already has plenty of blankets. I really don't think we need any more," I tried to reason.

"Oh crumbs, Olive! I need some for my house when the baby

spends the night. I'm getting them," she informed me as she tucked them under her arm and turned her focus on some Noah's Ark crib sheets.

We continued shopping at an unrushed pace, gathering more things we probably didn't need until my hip started aching as it usually did after a lot of walking. I tried rubbing it out with my hand, but it was shooting down my leg. My doctor had mentioned that it was my sciatic nerve, and that when it acted up, I needed to rest. Eyeing a bench—probably designed for tired pregnant women—I plopped down and sighed.

"Olive, baby, is your hip bothering you again?" Connie asked, concerned. She sat down beside me and regarded me with worried eyes.

"Yeah, it's my hip. I'm sorry, but we may need to go," I groaned as I tried to stretch my leg out for relief. My top was stretched across my now very large belly, so when the baby kicked out, my stomach contorted into an unusual position.

"Hi there, little one. Do you hear Granny's voice?" she fussed over me as her hand stroked the area of my belly where a foot prominently poked out. Connie winked knowingly at me. "He's going to have big feet like his daddy."

Funny thing was that we had no idea the sex of the baby— hence the green and yellow color scheme—but Connie and Bray were both convinced our child was going to be a boy. Bray and I couldn't decide on names either way—it would be a race to the birth certificate.

When my phone started to play Pepper's ringtone, I hurried and fished it out of my purse.

"Hey, Pepper," I greeted.

In true Pepper style, she launched into what she'd called for. "Opal has it bad for Trent. I met Jordan and my daddy at the office for lunch today since there was a board meeting, and of course Trent was there. Their meeting held over, and right before they came out of the board room, I watched her unbutton two of her blouse buttons. Once he passed by her desk, she called him over and asked him about the weather or some shit. I swear I watched his eyes bug out of his fucking head when he realized her boobs were hanging out. It was hard not to laugh my ass off watching him try to keep his eyes on hers. She was torturing him—I'm pretty sure Andi taught her some tricks. Did you know she had it bad for him?"

I laughed as I realized that I should have known something was going on with Opal. A few weeks ago, she'd informed me that she wanted to take some finance classes next semester. Now I understood that it had to do something with possibly impressing Trent. He had to be pushing thirty, while she was almost nineteen. I wasn't sure how I felt about their age difference. Maybe it was just a crush.

"She hasn't told me that she likes him, but she might think I wouldn't approve of her dating an older man. Ugh, she is so sneaky. I was just there last night at her apartment and she didn't say a word about her feelings towards him. I'll call her tonight and get the scoop. You're a good little spy, Pepper," I teased.

Changing the subject, she groaned, "Girl, my cravings are so fucking bad lately. Last night, I woke Jordan up at three in the morning because I really wanted some spaghetti. Who the hell sells spaghetti at that time of night, right? My poor husband had to find a grocery store that was open twenty-four hours and buy all the ingredients. He came back home, dead tired, and made me spaghetti. Once he dished it up for me, I suddenly wasn't feeling it anymore. I opted for a banana instead. I think he might divorce me over this pregnancy and we've barely been married five months."

I giggled at her, knowing that man would never divorce her. He was completely head over heels in love with her and their growing little girl. They'd already decided to call her Mia. I was envious of the quick decision they both happily agreed upon—unlike Bray and me, who couldn't decide on anything. He still called his "son" A.B.

"You're a mess, Pepper. Are we still on for lunch tomorrow?" I asked as I eased myself off the bench.

"Yes, but I can't pick a placc until right before we go. I have no fucking clue what will sound good until that exact moment," she laughed.

Once we hung up and I had stood, I told Connie, "I'm going to find a restroom while you check out. I'll meet you downstairs when I'm finished."

She nodded and headed off toward the counter while I set out to find the restrooms. A few minutes later, I made my way to the stairwell since it was closer and only one flight of stairs. My doctor had told me that I needed to exercise anyway. I'd just stepped in and got ready to go down the steps when someone quickly came in after me and shocked me by grabbing my hair.

I was pulled backwards, and before I could scream, a large hand covered my mouth. My heart pounded wildly in my chest as I came to the realization that I was in the clutches of none other than Drake himself.

"Look at you, Ollie. You've gained weight but you're still as beautiful as always. I've waited so long to take you back home with me," he breathed into my ear.

A shiver rattled through me as I tried to recall some of my self-defense training where we learned how to escape an attacker. Things were a lot harder while pregnant and achy though. My fingers scratched at his hand over my mouth in an attempt to get him to let go. His hand that held me to him slid down to splay across my belly.

"We're going to be so happy together—you, me, and our baby," he attempted to assure me. I could feel a scream building in my throat as I panicked about his delusional thoughts. All that could escape were tearful whimpers.

If only I could get to my purse, which was now on the floor, I could access my gun, which was stowed away for this very reason.

"I've missed you so much, Ollie. I'm a changed man—I would never put my hands on you again," he promised into my ear, gently biting my lobe.

In that moment, all I could think about was saving my baby. My sweet little A.B. growing inside. Bray's baby. In that instant, I raised my foot and stomped on his foot hard. Using my training from my self-defense classes, I seized the opportunity when he cursed and released me to elbow him forcefully in the gut. I bolted toward the stairs and had just reached the first one when I was yanked once again by my hair.

"Let go of me!" I screeched and attempted to free myself from his grip.

"Have it your way," he growled and violently shoved me toward the steps.

It was in that moment that my hip decided to send searing pain down my leg and give out, causing me to collapse. I attempted to reach out for anything to grab on to but was unsuccessful and hit the first steps hard on my knees and then elbows. Gravity took over and I rolled down the stairs, hitting hard the entire way down.

When I reached the bottom, agonizing pain burned through my abdomen. With shaky hands, I gently stroked my belly. *Please be okay. Please be okay.* Glancing back up the stairwell, I realized that Drake had disappeared. Wincing, I looked around for my purse to see if I could find my phone. I didn't find it but I did finally notice a quickly growing pool of blood on the floor between my legs. *Oh God, no. Not again.* Agony and despair took over, making me black out.

Chapter TWENTY-NINE

Bray

"WE GOT THE Jamison account," Jackson grinned and plopped down at my desk.

Funny how things in your life could drastically change. It wasn't long ago that we'd hated each other and could barely stand to be in the same room. When we'd been in Vegas and he'd nearly ruined my relationship with Olive, I'd pretty much hated his guts then as well. But somehow over time, we'd grown to like each other. I still liked to give him shit about his Harry Potter obsession, which we'd all found out about after Andi had blabbed it one day when she was drunk.

I smiled back at him and slapped down some new blueprints in front of him. "What do you think about these for the Madsen building on Fifth?" I asked.

My phone rang on the desk beside me. Seeing that it was my mom probably calling to give me a recap of her shopping trip, I ignored the call.

"Wow, dude. This turned out fucking awesome," Jackson praised as he flipped through the plans.

My phone rang again immediately after, meaning she hadn't left a voicemail. Thinking about Olive getting closer to her due date, I answered.

"Hey, Mom, what's up?" I asked as I leaned over and pointed at a section of the blueprints I wanted Jackson to see.

"Bray, honey, you need to get to the hospital. Right now. Olive fell down the stairs," she sobbed into the phone.

My entire body went cold. "What? Is she okay?" I demanded as I scooped up my keys from my desk and stood.

"She's in surgery—she was hemorrhaging. Oh my God, Bray, there was so much blood. I think I'm going to be sick," she wailed. I suddenly could hear her vomiting on the other line.

"Mom, I'll be right there," I promised and hung up.

Jackson, sensing the gravity of the situation, had already stood.

"Olive's in surgery. She fell down the stairs," I choked out as I shakily made my way to the door.

"Come on. George can drive us," he told me calmly. "Andi, Opal, we're going to the hospital—now!" he shouted at them.

Both girls rounded the corner with horrified looks, realizing that it meant Olive was hurt.

We were in the elevators before anyone said anything.

"What's wrong with her, Bray?" Opal asked tearfully.

"And is the baby okay?" Andi chimed in right after.

"I don't know. Mom said she fell down the stairs. She said there was—oh God. She said there was blood everywhere," I wheezed out. Running my hands through my hair, I fought to keep from crying. My Olive and our little A.B. were in trouble. It made me fucking sick to think about it.

Andi rushed over to me and enveloped me in a comforting hug, which succeeded in releasing my tears.

"Shh, Bray. Olive is a fighter. She'll be okay," she promised as she stroked my back in an effort to soothe me.

When the elevators opened, we all rushed out to the car, where George was waiting. Piling in, I tried not to think about what was going to happen. Olive was my world, and we already loved our little baby. If something happened to either one of them, I would be destroyed.

Minutes later, we pulled up to the hospital, and I was the first to jump out, bolting inside. Mom was waiting in the lobby area for us, looking quite ashen. Dad was behind her, stroking her back. For Dad to have come up here, things must have been bad.

"Oh, honey," she began tearfully.

"What? Mom, where is she? What's going on?" I demanded quickly.

"Baby, she's in surgery. That's all the information they have for us right now. I'm so sorry," she cried and hugged me tight.

Pulling from her, I sat down in a chair with my elbows on my knees. *Please, God, let her and the baby be okay.* I wasn't sure how much time had passed with me staring at the floor, but suddenly Pepper knelt in front of me. When had she gotten here?

"Bray, Olive is a fighter. She always has been and always will be. The girl is as sweet as they come, but she's made of the tough stuff. I know she'll pull through," she promised.

Pregnancy must be playing with Pepper's emotions, because I'd never seen such a compassionate, caring look on her face directed at me. Not once—ever. The kindness in her eyes killed me. She stood up and pulled me to my feet so she could hug me. Her swollen belly between us was enough to send me over the edge, and loud sobs escaped my throat.

"Bray, I'm sorry," she whispered as she hugged me tight. "I've never treated you like you deserve to be treated. Your love for Olive is so evident. It shines in your eyes—a shine I've only ever seen when you look at her. Please forgive me for being a bitch. I just love my two girls very much and would do anything to protect them."

Squeezing her tight, I kissed the top of her head, tears rolling into her hair. "I know, Pepper. Thank you."

Releasing me, she affixed her bitch face and stormed over to the desk. "What the hell is taking so long? When will someone give us some answers? My friend over there is worried to death over his girlfriend and baby. Now who is going to fucking give us some answers?!"

Andi attempted to calm her down. "Pepper, it's okay. They're doing their job."

"Andi, we've been here for four fucking hours without a single word on her condition," she fumed but allowed Andi to pull her back to the seating area.

"We've been here for four hours?" I asked still somewhat dazed. Looking around, I found that Mom and Dad were missing.

Opal was curled up in her chair fast asleep. Jackson and Jordan were both sitting side by side, looking on their phones.

"Where are my parents?" I asked Pepper and Andi, who had come to stand in front of me.

"Your dad took your mom home. She had gotten herself so worked up that she had a migraine. He practically had to drag her out of here though because she didn't want to leave you. They told you goodbye but you were in your zone," Andi told me softly.

"Are you the family of Olive Redding?" a voice asked us.

Swiveling toward the voice, I stalked over to the female doctor. She looked quite drained, and my stomach dropped.

"She'll be my wife soon and she's the mother of my baby," I confirmed softly. *Please, God, let her be okay.* She wanted to wait until we'd had the baby to get married, but I'd been ready since the day she moved in with me. If I lost the woman who was supposed to be my wife, I would never recover.

"My name is Dr. Winston. Sir, can we speak privately?" she asked quietly, eyes darting over at Andi and Pepper beside me.

"It's okay, just tell me now. Is she okay? Is the baby okay?"

"Sir, we managed to stop the bleeding and she is now stabilized in ICU. But I'm afraid she had some complications. Since she was eight months pregnant—"

Complications? Was eight months pregnant as in no longer pregnant with our baby? My stomach dropped as my knees weakened, and I fell to them. *Not our baby.*

Losing all focus of what she was saying, I thought back to the first time I felt little A.B. move in her belly a couple of months ago.

"Bray, hurry!" Olive screeched.

Afraid that she was hurt, I ran out of the bathroom still dripping wet from my shower with my towel tied around my waist.

"What is it, baby? Are you okay?" I asked, coming to her bedside.

Instead of answering me, she snatched my hand and brought it to her belly. At first, I didn't feel anything, but suddenly something bumped my palm. My eyes flew to hers.

"Is that A.B. kicking?" I asked excitedly.

She nodded with a huge grin on her face. I kissed her belly where my baby just kicked and was awarded another soft kick to my lips this time.

"Hey there, little guy. Daddy loves you," I told my son. When I peeked up at Olive, she rolled her eyes but was still smiling. She thinks it is silly for me to call the baby a boy when we have no idea of the sex. This was our first real family moment, and my heart swelled with pride. Trailing kisses up her bare, scarred belly, I made my way up to her now larger breasts. I pulled up her tank and freed her breasts, taking one into my mouth.

"Oh, Bray," she moaned softly. Suddenly my towel was pulled from my waist.

Noticing the heat in her eyes, I stood up and slid her panties down her legs. After I tossed them on the floor, I climbed onto the bed and sat on my knees, admiring her beauty. Her eyes fell to my cock and she bit her lip.

Spreading her legs, I brought my face to her sweet pussy, dragging my tongue up her slit.

"Bray," she moaned and gripped onto my hair.

Using my thumbs, I spread her apart to give myself better access. Diving in again so I could enjoy the taste of her, I began the series of swirls and flicks that I knew drove her crazy. Within minutes, she was screaming my name and losing control beneath me. I would never grow tired of giving this beautiful woman orgasms.

Sitting up, I brought my cock between her legs and teased her wet entrance with the tip. She wrapped her long legs around me and urged me closer by digging her heels into my back. Careful not to hurt her, I slowly sank myself into her swollen heat. Recently, she'd become insatiable with our lovemaking. The doctor told us that it was normal and that she might experience more pleasure due to the increased blood flow in that area. Boy was she right.

Once I was completely seated inside her, I leaned over and kissed her lips. Her belly had gotten just big enough to poke mine while we made love. As our tongues intertwined and teased each other, I thrust into her slowly.

"I love you, Olive," I groaned against her lips as my orgasm quickly made its way to me.

"I love you too, Bray," she mewled as a shudder passed through her.

Her pussy clenched tightly around my dick, indicating her climax, which pushed me over the edge. My own hot release shot into her. We happily rode out the aftershocks together while little A.B. kicked me through her belly, making us both chuckle.

"Bray?" Andi asked quietly, pulling me from my memories. Memories that only seemed like yesterday.

I was still on my knees, but the doctor no longer stood before me. Andi had pulled a chair over to me and was sitting in it, patting my back.

"How is Olive? Where did the doctor go?" I demanded, my

voice rising as I realized I'd completely zoned out on the doctor.

"She's stable. We can see her soon. Dr. Winston said they did the best they could to save—"

And once again, I completely checked out, not wanting to hear the words.

Chapter Thirty

Olive

MY THROAT WAS so dry. If only I could get something to drink. What was that beeping noise I was hearing? I felt like I'd been hit by a bus. Dragging my eyes open, I took a moment to adjust to my scenery. I was in a hospital room. Had I had the baby? Bray was sprawled out on the small sofa in the room, snoring softly.

Glancing down at my flattened belly under the sheets, I suddenly felt sick as I remembered Drake and the fall down the stairs. If I'd had the baby, wouldn't there be people everywhere congratulating me? Where was my baby? The monitors started beeping loudly and a nurse rushed in to my side.

"Hi there, young lady. I'm your nurse, Heather. How are you feeling?" she asked as she came over to my bedside.

Ignoring her gentle greeting, I launched right into my questions. "Where's my baby? Is my baby okay?" I rasped out.

Frowning, she patted my leg before heading to the door. "Dr. Winston wanted to talk to you when you woke up. I'm going to go grab her real quick and let her explain what happened."

Explain what happened? *God, no. Not again.* Tears rolled down my face, and I was helpless to stop them. A silent sob escaped me, and I felt pain in my abdomen. My poor baby. Little A.B.

Dr. Winston walked back over to the bed, a somber look on her face. Turning away from her, I focused on Bray, who was still sleeping on the sofa. His large body seemed to swallow the little sofa underneath him. The way his long legs hung off the end normally would have had me laughing. But not today.

"Miss Redding, do you know what happened?" she asked gently.

I forced my gaze back to her, not wanting to hear the words she had to say.

"My ex, Drake, pushed me down the stairs," I whispered, once again looking over at Bray.

"I was afraid of that, honey. Remember, I was on your case last time you were here. Listen, I need to tell you something. When you fell, your uterus tore and you hemorrhaged badly. Because of that, you required surgery and a blood transfusion. We nearly lost you on the table, Miss Redding. It's a miracle you are even alive after all the blood loss. However, we did have a major complication. We had to remove—"

My wails cut her off. I couldn't hear about how she'd had to remove my dead child. It would mean it was finally real. She was speaking rapidly, trying to calm me down, but all I could think about was my little A.B. Two large hands gently stroked my wet cheeks and lifted my face. Bray's teary eyes met my own.

"God, baby, I was so worried about you. I love you so much, Olive. I would have been destroyed had anything happened to you," he told me and kissed my lips. Everything about him served to comfort me. His voice. His smell. His touch.

"Bray, I'm sorry. He took another baby from me. I hate him," I sobbed.

"Shit, Olive. I'm so sorry. I was so worried about you that I didn't even mention our baby. Olive, she's safe. She's in the nursery waiting for Mommy to wake up. Even though she came a little earlier than we expected, she was far enough along that she'll be fine. Babe, she's absolutely beautiful," he grinned, eyes shining with pride.

"She? My baby is safe? I don't understand," I told him confusedly and brought my gaze back to Dr. Winston.

She sat on the side of my bed and took hold of my hand, much like a mother should in this sort of situation. "Miss Redding, I was trying to explain to you that we had to remove your uterus during surgery. It was damaged beyond repair. Your baby girl is perfect but I'm incredibly sorry—you won't be able to conceive again."

My heart sank at the prospect of never having any more children again. But when I thought about how my child was safe, I pushed through the pain. At least I had my little girl.

"I want to see her," I whispered to her as tears fell down my cheeks.

She squeezed my hand and smiled before leaving the room.

"Olive?" Bray asked. Turning to him, I could see worry etched all over his face. "What do you mean he took another baby from you?"

Shame poured over me. I had wanted to carry that secret to my grave, but now I had to tell him. "That night that he carved me and beat me severely, I managed to escape. The hospital stitched me up, but they told me I was pregnant and had lost the baby. I couldn't protect my baby from him. Just like today."

Fury painted his face as he growled his next words. "Just like today? What do you mean just like today? Olive, did he push you down the stairs?" He was scowling and his jaw clicked furiously as he waited for my explanation.

"He accosted me in the stairwell. I was able to free myself, but then he shoved me down the stairs. Bray, I can't live my life always worrying about if he will try to hurt me or our baby," I sighed.

"He's going down for this, baby. I promise." The look on his face told me that I could wholeheartedly believe him.

"Miss Redding, we have a surprise for you," the nurse named Heather chirped as she wheeled in a cart into our room. She picked up a bundled little thing wearing a pink stocking cap.

My heart fluttered as I realized I was about to hold my little baby. I flicked my gaze over to Bray, whose face was overcome with joy.

She pulled a tiny foot from the blanket to reveal a bracelet on my baby's ankle. "Hold your wrist up," she instructed. I did as I was told, and when our bracelets came near one another, they made a musical chime, indicating that she was definitely my baby. But as Heather carefully transferred my baby to my arms, my heart knew she was all mine—no bracelets needed.

"She's beautiful," I whispered as tears filled my eyes. Quickly, I blinked them away so I could see her better.

Her skin was lighter than my chocolate-colored flesh but darker than Bray's. She was the color of coffee with cream. Perfect. I grinned as I marveled at her hair. She had so much of it. It was a pale brown color—again, a perfect blend of Bray and me.

Bringing my lips to her forehead, I kissed her softly. "Abigail Constance Greene." It wasn't a question or a request—it was an announcement of her name. In that moment, it had just come to me. We'd been calling her A.B. ever since the first ultrasound, so Abby was a fitting nickname. And she would be named after her Granny as well.

"I love it, babe. It's a beautiful name for a beautiful girl," he praised and carefully stroked her soft hair.

Her face scrunched up at the sound of his voice, and she squinted open her eyes. We gasped at how pale blue they were— such a contrast to her skin.

"I'm going to have to buy a shotgun," he chuckled. She would most definitely grow to be strikingly exotic and unique.

This moment was perfect—just the three of us. And it lasted all of two seconds before someone burst in the door.

"Aunt Pepper's here!" Pepper announced, her arms full of shopping bags. "Once we found out you had a girl, I couldn't bear for my niece to wear some stupid green and yellow shit. I come bearing gifts—gifts of the pink, frilly variety."

Bray and I chuckled as she set her bags down on the couch and hurried over to us. Jordan followed inside with more sacks.

"Pepper, you shouldn't have. Really," I told her.

She waved me away and bent over to get a closer look at Abby. "Oh, Olive. She's gorgeous! Who's the dad?" she teased, winking at Bray. He chuckled from beside me. Things with them seemed lighter. I guess bringing a baby into the picture will do that to you.

Moments later, Andi and her real aunt Opal came in along with Jackson. The girls all tried to quiet their squeals, but it was hard not to get excited. Abby slept peacefully in my arms while everyone chatted away happily, crammed into the small rom. Bray kissed her forehead and then mine before ushering Jackson and Jordan out into the hallway.

The door opened again and Connie flew in with a grin that stretched across her face.

"Oh, Olive, she's precious. I can see so much of my Brayden in her. You did well, kid," she told me and winked.

"Her name's Abigail Constance. Would you like to hold her?" I asked.

Her eyes misted as she realized we'd named Abby after her. Nodding happily, she took her from my arms and snuggled her close.

"Hi there, sweet baby girl. Granny is going to spoil you rotten," she purred as she rocked her granddaughter. Abby let out a sigh and we all laughed.

The guys came back inside, all frowning, but once Bray made

it back over to my bed, he shone with happiness once again. I let him kiss me, and I once again marveled at my perfect little family.

Chapter THIRTY -ONE

Bray

AFTER EVERYONE LEFT for the evening and Olive was asleep, I called Jordan as I slipped out of the room.

"Hey, what did your father-in-law say?" I asked him as I sat down in a chair outside the room.

"He talked to his PI that he used for Elizabeth when Cole was stalking her and he's already been digging. Turns out, Drake has been missing a lot of photo shoots he's been scheduled for. Just yesterday, one of his bigger contracts was discontinued because of that. The PI said that people were saying he's been a loose cannon as of late. One of the younger models hasn't shown up for work in days. Do you think Drake could have her? Are you going to call the police?" he asked.

I rubbed my free hand through my hair. I'd never considered that Drake might just keep doing evil shit to women. Once we rescued Opal from his clutches, I'd hope that had been the end of it. I had always assumed that he was just obsessed with Olive.

"Jordan, why don't you call your father-in-law since he's chummy with the judges and see if they can get a search warrant. I'll call my contact at the police station that we talked to last time Drake harassed Olive. It doesn't sit well with me that this fucker tried to kill my girlfriend and my daughter and is walking around a free man. With the other model missing, that fucker might just have her stowed away like he had done with Opal and Olive. It would be ideal if we could catch the asshole in the act. They'd surely put his ass away and without bail. Call your father-in-law and I'll call my contact. Text me after. Thanks, Jordan. You're a good friend."

After I hung up, I snuck back into the room. Olive's nurse had come in and given her something for the pain, so she was completely out of it. We had sent Abby back to the nursery so she could sleep. Kissing Olive softly on the forehead, I slipped back out of the room and headed to the police station.

"Baby, wake up," I whispered against Olive's lips.

She blinked them open and smiled as she kissed me. "You're up early, and I see you've already sent for Abby," she giggled. Abby was drinking from the bottle I was holding. We'd already spent most of the morning staring at each other. I loved the way she would scrunch up her nose whenever I would talk to her. She'd been around for less than twenty-four hours and she was already my whole world.

After she finished the bottle and I burped her like her nurse Heather had shown me, I put her in Olive's arms. Olive gazed lovingly at our daughter.

"Babe, I have good news," I began, barely able to contain my excitement.

She kissed Abby and looked up at me, waiting for me to go on.

"He's in jail without bail," I beamed at her.

"Who? Drake? How?" she asked, shocked.

Grinning at her, I sat down and stroked her cheek. "Olive,

last night, a lot of people worked together to put him away. After talking with the police with Opal, they were able to use Pepper's dad's connection and get ahold of a judge really late who signed off on a search warrant. The police arrested him once they found a beaten woman tied to his bed. There's so much evidence stacked against him. He'll be going to jail for a long time." I left out the part where they had found an entire wall of photos of her in the spare room—the fucker had even had a copy of our sonogram. It chilled me to know how he'd obtained that.

Her eyes filled with tears and she grinned broadly at me. "I love you, Brayden Greene. From that moment you walked into my life, I've been smitten. Thank you for being exactly what I need and more than I ever wanted."

I brought my face close to hers and captured her mouth with mine. Our tongues danced together before I sucked on her lip and pulled away to look at her.

"Olive, I love you too. I vow to always protect you girls. You both are my whole world. And as soon as we get out of this place, you're going to marry me," I informed her.

She giggled, but it died in her throat when I pulled out the ring I'd picked out several weeks ago and eased it on her finger.

"Olive Redding, will you marry me?" I whispered simply and kissed her chastely on her lips.

One word changed my life forever. She kissed me deeply before finally giving me my answer.

"Yes."

Epilogue

Olive

Six weeks later…

"**I NOW PRONOUNCE** you husband and wife. You may kiss your bride," the judge told us.

We'd opted for a simple wedding at the courthouse, but it was perfect. Bray brought his hands to my neck and pulled me to him. His lips met mine with a gently urgency, marking me as his wife. I fingered the chain around my neck until I found the angel wings and rubbed them. Not long after we'd gotten home from the hospital, Bray had given me the necklace in memory of the baby I had lost. It was the best gift I had ever received from anyone.

Abby cried out from Connie's lap. She had fallen asleep before the ceremony, and I'd worried she might wake up starving right in the middle of it. But like the good little girl she was, she had waited until afterwards to make a peep. She truly was a little angel, and she hardly ever gave us any trouble.

We broke our kiss, and Bray went over to Connie to get his baby girl. "Hey there, Princess Abby. Did you miss Daddy?" he cooed. He got too close to her hands because she seized his hair and devoured his nose—clearly she was quite hungry.

I hurried over and freed him from her surprisingly strong

grip. When she saw that I had picked her up, she rewarded me with an adorable grin that melted my heart, just like it always did. My life was now complete with my sweet daughter and husband.

"Motherfucker! What in the hell?" Pepper shouted from where she was seated, reminding me that there were actually people in the room besides the two stars I orbited around. In fact, everyone I cared for was in that room.

"What is it, Pepper?" I asked, but when she stood up, I knew.

"Fuck! Shit! I can't do this. Jordan, I can't do this!" she screeched, her voice rising quickly.

He'd already stood and put his arms around her. "Calm down, babe. Your water broke. Mia is on her way," he grinned happily.

Andi and I squealed. We were so happy for Pepper to be having a baby—it would have been even more perfect if Andi had been pregnant too. But so far, no such luck in the baby department for her and Jackson.

"Oh my God!" Pepper howled as she clutched her midsection as a labor pain sliced through her. Jordan had a grip on her elbows so she wouldn't hit the floor. His smile was gone and he looked thoroughly freaked out.

"Come on, baby. Let's get you to the hospital," he told her urgently as he ushered her out of the small room.

"So, I guess lunch is off?" Jackson questioned innocently.

Before Andi could take his head off, Opal who was standing beside him punched him in the arm.

Glaring at her, he rubbed his arm while Andi laughed with Opal.

"You can eat from the hospital vending machine," Opal informed him as the three of them trailed after Jordan and Pepper.

Walking over to Bray, I clasped my free hand with his, and together, the three of us left to begin our life—well, right after we meet our new niece first.

The End.

The Practical Joke

I'm a jokester and like to mess with my friends. My most recent joke was one I played on my beta readers and editor. I slipped in this fake epilogue right before the real one you just finished reading. The results were hilarious. Words like "YOU BITCH" and "I thought I was going to have to come to Oklahoma to beat you up" and "I told my grandma you ruined a whole series in one chapter" were just a few of the messages I received. It was quite hysterical. You, as my reader, get to read the fake epilogue I tricked them with. I'm still grinning like a loon. Enjoy and I hope you get a good laugh!

Epilogue

Bray

One year later...

"SHHHHH, ABBY IS ASLEEP," I whispered into her neck before nipping at it, making her yelp again. These were stolen moments, and we needed every second alone.

"Oh, God, I missed this. It seems like forever since the last time we made love," she said before pressing her lips to mine. And it had been. It was probably a week ago that we'd been able to slip in a quickie at the office when I'd had to stay late.

I pushed up her skirt around her hips and growled when I realized she wasn't wearing panties. It was the hottest fucking thing in the world.

"Come here, sexy woman," I ordered and lifted her by her ass. She wrapped her legs around me as I sank my cock into her wet pussy. Leaning her against the wall for support, I pounded into her.

"Oh, Bray, you feel so good," she moaned against my lips.

"God, baby, so do you. I'm about to come—my cock has missed this sweet pussy."

I could feel myself coming undone and worried whether or not she would come as well, but when I felt her clenching around my dick, I knew we'd arrived together. My hot release spurted into her.

Kissing her chastely on the lips, I pulled out of her and brought my pants up. "We need to hurry. We don't have much time," I reminded her.

Skipping happily into the bathroom, she cleaned herself up and met me minutes later.

"Bray, I love you so much. I want this all the time. The only time I'm happy is with you. What are we going to do?" she asked sadly.

"Andi, I love you too. We'll figure it out. But for now, we'll keep stealing moments when we can, babe," I told her.

She smiled at me, and I quickly ushered her out of the apartment before Olive came back home. *(Just kidding! Do you think I would really do that to you? Bray loves Olive and Andi loves Jackson. I just wanted to freak you out. Continue on for the real epilogue. Laughing my ass off....)*

Mistake

(Breaking the Rules, Book 4)

Coming soon!

Prologue

Opal's first day of college…

You were a mistake. That was a constant reminder in my home growing up. Momma took every chance she could to remind me of just that. A mistake for her getting pregnant from a loser? A mistake for her not getting an abortion or putting me up for adoption?

My entire life has been one big mistake. Every decision I make always ends up being the wrong one. In high school when I joined a drama class just because I thought the teacher was hot, that was a mistake. Turns out, I couldn't act and the teacher hated that I was the worst one in the group. Both he and the class took their digs at me daily about how horrible I was. *It was a fucking nightmare.*

When I decided to get a job at a restaurant waiting tables so I could save to go see Olive in New York, that too was a mistake. After spilling coffee all over three customers in a single day, I was fired. Apparently I wasn't cut out for that sort of work.

At eighteen, when a fine ass black man showed up on my doorstep offering to whisk me away to New York City so I could model, well that was a mistake as well. Turns out, my naïve ass moved in with a psychopathic, sadistic shithead that was obsessed with my sister and just using me to get to her. Big mistake. *Huge.*

I'm tired of making mistakes. Once I set my eyes on the handsome investment banker, Trent Sutton, I knew things were going to turn around for me. In an effort to quit making mistakes and make something of myself, I chose to enroll at CUNY and get my Bachelor's degree in Investment Banking. That would get Trent to notice me.

For once, I was going to learn from my mistakes and start making better decisions. Things were going to change. I could feel it.

My Books

The Breaking the Rules Series:
Broken (Book 1) – Available Now!
Wrong (Book 2) – Available Now!
Scarred (Book 3) – Available Now!
Mistake (Book 4) – Coming Soon!
Crushed (Novella 4.5) – Coming Summer 2014!
Disgrace (Book 5) – Coming Summer 2014!

The Vegas Aces Series:
Rock Country (Book 1) – Available Now!
Christmas at Caesar's Palace (Book 2) – Coming Fall 2014!

Apartment 2B (Standalone Novel) – May 2014!
Moth to a Flame (Standalone Novel) – Coming Soon!
Sweet Vengeance – Coming Soon!

Acknowledgements

Having a support group is the most amazing thing in the world. My support group is the ladies on the Breaking the Rules Babes street team. Those women are incredibly encouraging not only to me but to each other. Without their constant daily kind words, I would be lost. Thank you Abby, Alexandra, Star, Becca, Chelsea, Courtney, Dawn, Ella, Ellen, Erica, Heather, Holly, Jennifer, Lorena, Maree, Michelle, Natalie, Nikki, Rebecca, Wendy, Carolyn, Christina, Dawn, Dena, and Heather. You guys rock my socks off.

I also want to thank my beta readers, whom are also my friends. Holly Sparks, Leann Jester, Mandy Abel, Star Price, Erica Thompson, Heather Dahlgren, and Wendy Colby you guys provided AMAZING support and feedback. Pointing out areas that didn't work and gushing over parts you loved, you helped boost the confidence I needed to finish what I'd started. I can't thank you enough and look forward to sending you more of my stories in the future.

I most certainly wouldn't be where I was without the support of "my biggest fan" Heather Dahlgren. Heather, you are like my own personal cheerleader. Every day you give me the fuel to power forward. When I have low moments, you lift me up. If I doubt myself, you squash those fears. At times when I'm happy, you do the happy dance with me. I love you girl and couldn't have made it through some recent hard times without you. Thanks for being the best, Nurse Heather!

Mickey, my fabulous editor from I'm a Book Shark, you keep me on the straight and narrow. Whenever my story "pulls" to the left, you "pull" me right back. Throughout the series, you've kept my story consistent with the previous books, gently reminding me of what *really* happened. The funny feedback and comments you provide always have me grinning from ear to ear. My favorite theme throughout this book was, "You've used the word pulled three times in the paragraph before, twice in this sentence, and I see one coming up." Thank you for encouraging me to "pull" other words from my vocabulary. My books would be embarrassing without you giving them a good spanking to whip them into shape. Thank you for not just being an editor but being my friend. Love you, girl!

Thank you Stacey Blake for formatting my books and making them look gorgeous. I know you want to beat me with a stick every time you see how many chapters my stories have after I send them to you. But you love me anyway and I'm so thankful. One of these days I'll make up for it and send you a case of your favorite wine, Beringer White Zinfandel. Cheers!

A huge thanks goes out to my sexy husband, Matt. While at first you thought of this as a hobby, you now support this as my career. It means the world to me. Thank you for paying all the Paypal invoices because I'm too blond to figure out how. All those times you had to do laundry or pick up supper because I was writing, I appreciate it more than you will ever know.

Lastly, but certainly not least of all, thank you to the wonderful readers out there that are willing to hear my story and enjoy my characters like I do. It means the world to me! My heart swells happily every time a reader messages me to tell me how much they enjoyed my book and read it in one night. You guys are fab—cyber kisses and hugs to you all!

Check out these other amazing authors as well......

Tears of Tess by **Pepper Winters**

Prologue

Three little words.

If anyone asked what I was most afraid of, what terrified me, stole my breath, and made my life flicker before my eyes, I would say three little words.

How could my perfect life plummet so far into hell?

How could my love for Brax twist so far into unfixable?

The black musty hood over my head suffocated my thoughts, and I sat with hands bound behind my back. Twine rubbed my wrists with hungry stringed teeth, ready to bleed me dry in this new existence.

Noise.

The cargo door of the airplane opened and footsteps thudded toward us. My senses were dulled, muted by the black hood; my mind ran amok with terror-filled images. Would I be raped? Mutilated? Would I ever see Brax again?

Male voices argued, and someone wrenched my arm upright. I flinched, crying out, earning a fist to my belly.

Tears streamed down my face. The first tears I shed, but definitely not the last.

This was my new future. Fate threw me to the bastards of Hades.

"That one."

My stomach twisted, threatening to evict empty contents. Oh, God.

Three little words:

I was sold.

Chapter One

Starling

"Where are you taking me, Brax?" I giggled as my boyfriend of two years beamed his slightly crooked smile and plucked my suitcase from my hands.

We crossed the threshold of the airport and nerves of excitement fluttered in my stomach.

A week ago, Brax surprised me with a romantic dinner and an envelope. I grabbed him and squeezed him half to death when I pulled free two airplane tickets with the destinations blacked out by a marker.

My perfect, sweet boyfriend, Brax Cliffingstone was taking me somewhere exotic. And that meant connection, sex, fun. Things I sorely needed.

Brax had never been able to keep a secret. Hell, he was a shockingly bad liar—I caught his fibs every time when his sky-blue eyes darted up and to the left, and his cute ears blushed.

But, somehow, he kept quiet on the whole mysterious holiday. Like any normal twenty-year-old woman, I searched our apartment ruthlessly. Raiding his underwear drawer, the

PlayStation compartment, and all the other secret hidey-holes where he might've kept the real plane reservations. But, for all my snooping, I came up empty.

So, as I stood in the Melbourne airport, with a crazy happy boyfriend and nerves rioting in my heart, I could only grin like an idiot.

"Not telling. The check-in clerk can be the one to ruin my surprise." He chuckled. "If it were up to me, I wouldn't tell you until we arrived at the resort." He dropped the suitcase and dragged me toward him with a smirk. "In fact, if I could, I'd blind-fold you until we got there, so it would all be a complete surprise."

My core clenched as thoughts flared with hot images—sexy, sinful visions of Brax blindfolding me, taking me roughly, com-pletely at his mercy. *Oh, God, don't go there again, Tess. You were going to block thoughts like that, remember?*

Ignoring myself, I gasped as Brax's fingers grazed my flesh. I shuddered, and my sequined top became insubstantial.

"You could do that, you know?" I whispered, dropping my eyelids to half-mast. "You could tie me up...."

Instead of pouncing and kissing me like crazy for offering him the chance to dominate, Brax swallowed and looked as if I'd told him to slap me with a dead fish.

"Tess, what the hell? That's the third time you've quipped about bondage."

Rejection crushed, and I dropped my gaze. The tingles be-tween my legs popped like dirty bubbles, and I let Brax shove me back into the box where I belonged. The box labelled: perfect, innocent girlfriend who'd do anything for him, as long as it was in the dark and on my back.

I wanted a new label. One that said: girlfriend who will do anything to be tied, spanked, and fucked all over rather than adored.

Brax looked so disappointed and I hated myself. *I need to*

stop this.

I reminded myself for the three-hundredth time, that the sweet, wonderful relationship I had with this man was far more important than a bit of sexy play in the bedroom.

I mumbled, "It's been too long. Almost a month and a half." I remembered the exact date when the lacklustre sex, in good ole missionary, took place. Brax worked overtime, my uni course demanded a lot of brainpower, and somehow life became more important than a roll beneath the sheets.

He froze, looking around us at the hordes of people. "Great time to bring that up." He guided me to the side, glaring at a couple that came too close. "Can we talk about this later?" He ducked his head and kissed my cheek. "I love you, hun. Once we aren't so busy, *then* we can have more alone time."

"And this holiday? Will you take me like the girlfriend you adore?"

Brax beamed, enveloping me in a hug. "Every night. You wait."

I smiled, letting anticipation and happiness dispel my angst. Brax and I wanted different things in the bedroom department, and I hoped, prayed, got on my knees and begged, that I didn't ruin what we had because of it.

My blood simmered for things entirely *not* sweet. Things I didn't have the courage to say. Downright sinful things that amped my blood to lava and made me wet—and it wasn't chaste kisses.

Standing in his arms, in a public place, with that sexy smirk on his mouth, and hands on my waist, I trembled with a cocktail of need. This trip would be exactly what we needed.

He brushed his lips against mine, no tongue, and I had to squeeze my legs together to stop the vibrations threatening to overtake me. *Is there something wrong with me?* Surely, I shouldn't be this way. Maybe there was a cure—something to take the edge off my desires.

Brax pulled back, smiling. "You're gorgeous."

My eyes dropped to his shapely mouth, breathing faster. What would Brax do if I pushed him against the wall and groped him in public? My mind turned the fantasy into *him* pushing *me* hard against the wall, his thigh going between my legs, hands pawing, bruising me because he couldn't get close enough.

I swallowed, battling those far too tempting thoughts. "You're not so bad yourself," I joked, plucking his baby-blue t-shirt that matched his eyes so well.

I loved this man, but missed him at the same time. How was that possible?

Life wedged between us: the university course stole five days a week, not to mention homework, and Brax's boss landed a new building contract in the heart of the city.

Each month trickled into the next, and lovemaking became second fiddle to *Call of Duty* on PlayStation, and architectural sketching for the extra credit I'd signed up for.

But all of that would change. Our life together would improve, because I was going to seduce my man. I'd packed a few naughty surprises to show Brax what turned me on. I needed to do this. To save my sanity. To save my relationship.

Brax's fingers squeezed my waist and he stepped away, ducking down to grab the suitcases again.

If I wanted to seduce him, wasn't it best just to go for it? Planning and dreaming seemed wrong when he stood right in front of me.

I dropped my shoulder bag and grabbed the lapels of his beige canvas jacket, yanking him into me. "Let's join the mile-high club," I whispered, before crushing his mouth with mine. His eyes flashed as I leaned forward, pressing my entire body against his. *Feel me. Need me.*

He tasted of orange juice and his lips were warm, so warm.

My tongue tried to gain welcome, but Brax's hands landed on my shoulders, holding me at bay.

Someone clapped, saying, "You attack him, girl!"

Brax stepped back, looking over my shoulder at the by-stander. He dropped his eyes to mine, temper flashing. "Nice spectacle, Tess. Are we done? Can we go check in?"

Disappointment sat like a heavy boulder in my belly. He sensed my mood—like he always did—and gathered me into a hug again. "I'm sorry. You know how much I hate PDA's. Get me behind closed doors, and I'm all yours." He smiled, and I nodded.

"You're right. Sorry. I'm just so excited to go on holiday with you." I dropped my eyes, letting wild, blonde curls curtain my face. *Please, don't let him see the rejection in my eyes.* Brax used to say my eyes reminded him of dove's feathers as the white bird flew across the sky. He could be very poetic, my Brax. But I didn't want poetry anymore. I wanted… I didn't know what I wanted.

He chuckled. "You're right about being excited." He waggled his eyebrows, and together we headed to check-in. The girl who'd told me to attack him winked and gave me a thumbs up.

I smiled, hiding the residual pain that my attack didn't inspire the same reaction.

We joined the queue, and I glanced around. People milled like fish in a pond, darting and weaving around groups of waiting passengers. The vibe of an airport never failed to excite me. Not that I travelled a lot. Before the university course, I travelled to Sydney to study the architecture there, and sketch. I loved to sketch buildings. At ten years of age, my parents took my brother and me to Bali for a week. Not that it was fun going on holiday with a thirty-year-old brother, and parents who despised me.

Old hurt surfaced, thinking of them. When I moved in with Brax eighteen months ago, I drifted apart from my parents. After all, they were almost seventy years old, and focused on other 'important things', rather than a daughter who'd come twenty years too late. A dreadful mistake, as they loved to remind me.

They'd been so horrified at the pregnancy, they promptly sued the doctor for botching my father's vasectomy.

An old enemy: rejection, ruled my life. I supposed the desperation to connect with Brax was a way of confirming that *someone* wanted me. I didn't just want intimacy, I *needed* it. I needed to feel his hands on me, his body in mine. It was a craving that never left me in peace.

I blinked, putting the impossible together. I needed Brax to be rough because I needed to be *claimed*.

Oh, my God, am I that screwed up?

I followed Brax in a daze to the counter, and let him put the suitcase on the scales.

"Morning. Tickets and passports, please," the girl in her smart uniform said.

Fumbling with luggage tags, Brax asked, "Honey, can you give her our tickets? They're in my back pocket."

I reached around and pulled out a travel wallet from his baggy jeans pocket. Although twenty-three years old, Brax still dressed like a grungy teenager. I squeezed his butt.

His eyes flashed to mine, frowning.

I forced a bright smile, handing our documentation to the clerk. I didn't even check where we were headed, too focused on ignoring the twinges of sadness at not being allowed to grope my boyfriend. *Maybe I'm too sexual?* My fears were right. I was hardwired all wrong.

"Thank you." The girl's eyes dropped, showing heavily shadowed lids. Her brown hair, scraped back into a tight bun, looked plastic with so much hair spray. She bit her lip and pulled out a ream of tickets before checking our passports. "Do you want your bags checked all the way through to Cancun?"

Cancun? My heart soared. Wow. Brax outdid himself. I never

would've thought he'd travel so far from home. I turned and kissed his cheek. "Thank you so much, Brax."

His face softened as he captured my hand. "You're welcome. There's no better way to celebrate our future, than going to a country that values friendship and family." He leaned closer. "I read that on Sundays the streets come alive with strangers dancing. Everyone becomes connected by music."

I couldn't tear myself from his crisp blue eyes. That was why I loved him, despite not being completely satisfied. Brax suffered the same insecurities. He didn't have anyone but me. His parents died in a car accident when he turned seventeen; he was an only child.

Brax owned the apartment we lived in, thanks to the life insurance pay out, and his dad's husky, Blizzard, came with the bargain.

Blizzard and I didn't see eye to eye, but Brax loved the dog like a tatty teddy-bear. I tolerated the beast, and kept my handbags far from chewing height.

"You're the best." I captured his chin, planting a kiss, not caring he was uncomfortable. Hell, the couple beside us were practically dry humping; a peck on the mouth was PG stuff.

The girl sighed across the counter. "Is this your honeymoon? Cancun is amazing. My boyfriend and I went there a few years ago. So hot and fun. And the music is so sexy, we couldn't keep our hands off each other."

Images filled my mind of twirling around Brax in a new sexy bikini. Maybe a change of scenery would amplify our lust.

I said, "No, not our honeymoon. Just a celebration."

Brax grinned, his eyes sparkling.

An idea ran wild. *Was* this trip special? Was Brax going to propose? I waited for the heart-flipping joy at becoming Mrs. Cliffingstone, but a swell of comfort filled me instead. I would say yes.

Brax wanted me. Brax was safe. I loved him in my own way—the way that mattered, the long-lasting kind.

Silence descended while the girl tap-tapped her keyboard and printed off our boarding passes. After tagging our bags, she handed everything back. "Your bags are checked all the way to Mexico, but you'll have a stop in Los Angeles for four hours." She circled the gate number and time. "Please make your way through immigration, and proceed to the departure lounge. You board at eleven-thirty."

Brax took the documentation and shouldered his laptop bag. Linking hands with me, he said, "Thank you."

We headed toward the Passengers Only lounge. We had little over an hour before boarding. I could think of a lot of things we could do in an hour, but I doubted Brax would be into them.

We were on our way to Mexico. A different country and a different bed awaited us. I could be patient.

I made up my mind as Brax browsed the tax-free PlayStation games that tonight would mark a new beginning for us. Goodbye contentment, hello lust.

Our relationship was going to rip and roar with love and flame. I would make sure of it.

Yes, tonight things would be different.

I needed different.

Picture Perfect by Ella Fox

Prologue

I was in no fucking mood to perform.

I was hung-over, or possibly still drunk, from a weeklong bender. I'd awakened to find three chicks in my hotel bed, which was *not* a great way to start the day. Most people would think that sounds like the best morning ever, and I admit the girls were hot, but the truth is, I hated waking up with people I didn't know. Combine that dislike with the fact that there were actually *three* people I didn't know in the bed, my brain felt like it was on fire, I couldn't remember what fucking city I was in *and* I was starving and you get an idea of why the morning sucked.

On top of all that, my dick felt as if it had gone twenty rounds with a bull that hadn't been gentle. In spite of the fact that I counted seven used condoms on the floor, I knew that I hadn't come. Story of my fucking life—I don't come with groupies, randoms, or people I didn't know. Since I hadn't fucked the same girl two nights in a row in years, I was used to it. As a rule, I survived by making myself come after the girls were gone, but clearly I hadn't taken care of business the night before and my package was paying the price.

The day continued to be shit and I wound up being late to sound check. My limo driver was an annoying prick that talked about himself the *entire* way to the stadium and I was ready to commit by the time I got there.

Still, I felt like shit that I was late, so I went in fully prepared to apologize. Turns out that I didn't have to bother because our bassist wasn't there and since no one knew where he was, my tardiness was overlooked. Our tour management tried to keep the three of us that were there calm by having an assistant go out to pick up food. The Philly cheesesteak I was handed was my clue that we were in Philadelphia. By my calculation, that meant I was three more months away from the end of this tour, and every one of those days seemed like it would stretch out for an eternity. I wanted to be fucking home, not waking up each morning playing a game I liked to call, "Where in the world am I today?" It's like *Where's Waldo*, but with groupies and hotel rooms.

Our bass player still hadn't shown by the time we finished eating and our moods weren't improving. Sound check was a major bust, but luckily, we had a dressing room filled with booze. Our tour rider stipulated a fully stocked bar at all of our shows, and this one didn't disappoint. With some hair of the dog, I was back to functioning normally in no time at all.

Unfortunately, I got a little too drunk, and that's why I was in no fuckin' mood to perform. It didn't help that the entire band was pissed at our bass player- now known as 'the asshole that shows up twenty minutes before a show'. We were all pretty wasted, but it didn't escape my notice that he was on something a hell of a lot stronger than alcohol.

The roar of the crowd as the lights went down in the stadium no longer excited me the way it used to, and that pissed me off too. What the fuck was wrong with me that I felt nothing good anymore? I was living what was supposed to be the dream life— and it was killing me, killing us all, really. Not one of us were happy or healthy, and it showed. We argued about fucking everything, something we'd never done before. I didn't know where we went wrong, but I was sick of it and I either needed to get the fuck out entirely or break out on my own. We'd made a pact—friends for life, brotherhood before business—but the brotherhood was waning and that made me angry.

I felt helpless. As the lead singer, wasn't it my job to keep my band on track? I knew that things were going off the rails with Tyson, knew that Gavin was in pain—but I couldn't do shit about it. I wasn't the man that I wanted to be, and I knew that if I kept going the way that I was, my life wasn't going to be worth shit. Life was only getting shorter and I wasn't happy—*none* of us were happy, at least not anymore. The last time I remembered being excited about what we were doing was before the band got sucked into the machine and became a commodity instead of a musical act.

I took the stage in a rage, mad at the world, mad at our management, mad at my band, but mostly, I was mad at myself for letting it all get this far. When I grabbed the mic I sang aggressively and gave the appearance of rocking, but I was phoning it in. I was in no mood so I gave myself a pass to fuck off since I knew it wasn't going to be a good show.

All that changed about four minutes in when I looked down into the front row and locked on to a pair of beautiful chocolate brown eyes. The girl was young, but she was stunning. She was singing along and smiling, and that made me feel like shit. She was there to rock, and there I was, phoning in bullshit.

Something about her, I can't even explain what, had me sick to my stomach even thinking about letting her down. She deserved better than whatever pathetic version of myself that I'd become. I used to really care about the fans and the experience, but for the last few years all I cared about was drinking, fucking and trying to feel something.

Staring into those eyes, I pulled my shit together and gave two and a half hours of a performance that was easily my best in years. I sang almost exclusively to her, the connection between us something I'd never experienced before. Over and over my conscience yelled *too young* in my head, and while I knew that to be true, I just wanted to fucking enjoy feeling something real for the first time in forever.

Unfortunately, she didn't get older during the show. When it was over, it was over, and reality took center stage again. The guitarist for our band, Cole, ribbed the fuck out of me as we left the stage after the encore, asking if I was going to give "jailbait" a backstage pass. I wasn't that big of an asshole, and I shook my head in the negative. "Fuck that, man. That would be too fucked up, even for me."

Grinning at me he said, "Dude, you should have seen yourself. I think that girl was your fucking Priscilla."

I glared at him as I shook my head in confusion. "Dude, what does that even mean? What the fuck is a Priscilla?"

He looked at me like I was some kind of a moron. "You really need to get your rock n' roll knowledge beefed up—you should know this without asking, it's like fuckin' music folklore. If we're ever on *Celebrity Jeopardy* and we lose because you don't know something this obvious, I'm going to kick your ass. I'm talking about Priscilla Presley, fuckwad. You totally went all Elvis over a teenage girl."

His words embarrassed me, mostly because they were true. I told him to fuck off and then I got the hell out of dodge.

It was humiliating to have gotten so turned on by a teenager. I guessed she was somewhere between sixteen and eighteen, but my brain said eighteen was probably a real fuckin' stretch. I was so disgusted with myself that I wound up getting blackout drunk in order to make it all go away.

* * *

I woke up feeling like shit again, but for the first time, I took stock of my situation and was honest with myself. I realized that I had to change the way I was living. I couldn't remember why, but I *knew,* down to my bones, that I needed to do better, to *be* better. I hadn't always been like a drunken robotic human dildo. I wanted to be worthy. Worthy of what, I couldn't say, but that was how I felt.

I didn't remember shit from the night before, but my band was happy to fill me in once I snapped out and demanded to know why everyone was calling me Elvis. Nothing they said sparked my memory. I could just barely remember eyes the color of melting chocolate, but that was all. No matter how much ribbing they did, nothing other than the eye color came back to me.

The name Elvis stuck for about six months, but I never got my memory back from the night that changed the path I was on forever.

Ignite by Tessa Teevan

Prologue

I fucking hate you sometimes…

The words replay in my head as if on loop. Like I've died and gone to Hell, where I'm tortured with those five cruel words over and over again. The words that came from the same lips that used to whisper "I love you" as he held me in the middle of the night. The lips that, at one point, couldn't wait to say "I do." Those beautiful lips I thought I'd spend the rest of my life kissing. "I fucking hate you…" Yep, definitely Hell.

Hell on Earth, that is. I'm still here. He's the one who's gone. The love of what I thought would be my life, the man I married, the one I was so sure I'd wake up to every single morning until the good Lord decided to bring me home. The same man, who, on what was unknowingly his last day, spoke those five heartless, torturous words he will never, ever get the chance to take back. That man's gone, and I'm still here, broken and alone.

I'm not a complete idiot. Just an overly dramatic one at times. I know my husband loved me. He'd loved me for more than seven years, and that didn't change. We just spent the morning lying in bed for a few extra minutes so we could be close. He fingered my hair as he told me he loved me and was looking forward to the weekend getaway we had planned. He wasn't going through the motions; he meant every word as he gave me a preview of what he had planned for our downtown Chicago hotel—if we ever decided to get out of bed and hit the road. It's just that I can be a raging psycho when I'm PMSing. Then throw in a wine hangover and I turn into Satan's worst nightmare. Every month it's either intense cramping for four days or my husband wonders where this crazy bitch stashed the sweet woman he married. Suffice it to say, I was not cramping this month.

I understood his frustrations with me when I was like that, and any other time I would've just ignored those words because I usually deserved them. I knew he'd end up doing something to make me laugh in the moments that followed because neither of us could stay mad for long. This was different. He'd never used the word hate before. It caught me by surprise, and at the time, I was extremely thankful for the sunglasses on my face as I looked out the window at the fields of towering windmills on the Indiana countryside.

Hate. I *hate* onions. I *hate* Ohio drivers in the winter. I *hate* anything sparkly-vampire related.

I hate a lot of things, I really do, but it's a strong emotion I only use when thinking about trivial things. My husband, though? Never, not once, have I ever felt hatred towards him, and it tore me in two to hear him say those words. And what's worse is that I'll never hear him say anything again.

We never did make it to Chicago. I don't remember much about that accident. Actually, I don't remember the accident at all. A car accident. I used to think that was so cliché. Couldn't life be a little more creative? And now, here I am, widowed at twenty-six because of a damn car accident I have no memory of, only splotchy nightmares that just give me snippets of what happened.

The eye witness and police reports say that a young college student was running late to get onto the Purdue campus for his early afternoon classes. He cut us off, clipping the front end of our car. We ended up spinning into oncoming traffic where we were hit by an SUV on the driver's side. He was killed instantly. I was knocked unconscious. When I woke up the next day in an Indianapolis hospital, I knew.

"Mrs. Tate, I wish we could have done something, but he was

killed on impact. Take solace in knowing that he felt no pain…"
The doctor continued, but his words were drowned out in my
mind, replaced by others.

I fucking hate you sometimes.

Made in the USA
Las Vegas, NV
26 December 2022

64137632R00125